WRONG PRINCE

AN ACCIDENTAL PREGNANCY ROMANCE

LILIAN MONROE

1

CARA

One difference between regular people and royalty is that regular people knock before entering your home.

Royals, on the other hand?

Knocking isn't part of their vocabulary.

The only warning I get that Prince Theo is at my house is the sound of a vehicle pulling up outside and the driver cutting the engine.

I assume it's one of my parents' friends or maybe a member of our household staff, and I ignore it.

The Crown Prince of Argyle bursts through the door in a blaze of abs and windswept hair, tearing the sunglasses off his bronzed face as he scans the room. A soft breeze follows after him, fluttering the edges of his linen shirt.

"Cara!" he calls out. I stand up, putting my book down on the sofa beside me. He flashes me a brilliant smile. "Come on. We're going."

Every word Theo speaks is a command. He was born a king, and a part of me likes when he speaks like that. There's something attractive about confidence and power, even though I'd never be caught dead saying that out loud.

I'm more of the 'don't tell me what to do' kind of gal—or at least that's what I tell myself. The fluttering in my belly begs to differ.

I frown. "Go where?"

The Prince's white linen shirt is unbuttoned, revealing his chiseled chest. He's wearing teal swimming trunks and a pair of white leather boat shoes. He nods toward the open door, grinning.

"It's the summer solstice. We have a tradition to uphold."

My heart thumps uncomfortably. I thought our traditions had died when Prince Luca's accident happened. That day, everything changed.

Three years ago, my betrothed, Prince Luca—Prince Theo's little brother—jumped off a cliff into shallow water and broke his back. Luca has been trying to recover from his injuries in Singapore, undergoing countless operations and hours of physical therapy.

And me?

I've been shut out. Languishing on the other side of the world. Begging him to talk to me, and then slowly accepting that it's over between us.

At first, I wanted to be there with him. The first year was hell. I called, and called, and called. I cried. I sent letters and messages. I sent him care packages and made sure to try to speak to him every day.

We have a special Post Office box, where we've been exchanging messages since we were kids. I checked it every day for a year, hoping he'd have sent me some note, some parcel, some sign that he cared.

Every day, it was empty.

Luca pushed me away. Slowly but surely, he stopped answering. The rest of the royal family backed away from me as my engagement to Luca fizzled. I didn't just lose my fiancé, I lost all my closest childhood friends.

Luca, Theo, Beckett, Dante—all four brothers became strangers to me. It nearly killed me.

I even went to Singapore a year after the accident, but Luca refused to see me.

The second year, I was in a daze. I don't remember much, except sleeping a lot and not eating much. The past three years have been the loneliest of my life.

It's only in the past six months that I've started coming around again. Slowly, I'm starting to feel like myself again. I'm making plans for the future. Plans for myself.

But Theo's standing here in front of me as if nothing at all has changed.

It *has* changed, though. Being pushed away by Luca is what finally made me decide to leave this Kingdom. I have to. It's the only way I can move on from all this.

Next week, I'm flying to the United States to pursue my dream of becoming a singer. I've applied to two dozen colleges for voice programs and haven't heard back from any of them, but that won't stop me. I'm done with letting people push me away and beat me down. I'm stronger than that. I've stared into the abyss, and now, I'm walking away.

I'll go to Los Angeles and work in a restaurant while I try to make it as a singer. I'll plead with record executives. I'll sing in dirty dive bars. I'll do whatever it takes, even if my parents think singing is beneath our family name.

I need to go. Do something for myself. Pursue a dream I've had since I was a little girl—a dream that predates Luca, and Theo, and all the heartache that the royal family brought me.

Knowing that I'm leaving is the only thing that has kept me going.

Up until two minutes ago, I thought I'd never see the Princes of Argyle again. I thought all four brothers had turned their backs on me after Luca's accident.

Apparently, I was wrong.

I clear my throat, combing my fingers through the ends of my long, brown hair. "Your Highness—"

"Cara," Theo huffs, shaking his head. "Come on. Stop standing there like we didn't spend every moment of our childhood together. Get your bathing suit on and get in my car. We're sailing around the islands."

Argyle is a Caribbean kingdom, complete with white, sandy beaches and waving palm trees. The Kingdom consists of about seventy islands, ranging from land masses the size of Cuba to small atolls with nothing but a single palm tree on them.

Nearly every year since I was seven years old, I've sailed around the Kingdom with the four Princes of Argyle. It takes just over two days to do it, and it's been a highlight of my year, every year, since I was a little girl.

Three years ago, our tradition abruptly stopped. Luca had just had his accident, and we didn't know whether he would recover. Sailing around the islands didn't seem right.

Our yearly sailing trip was yet another thing I mourned.

Prince Theo, the eldest of the Princes of Argyle, stares at me, eyebrows raised. "Well?"

"I thought..." I clear my throat. "I didn't think we were doing that anymore."

"Look, Luca might be refusing to talk to you, but it doesn't mean we aren't friends. We've done this every year since we were kids. It's tradition."

"Dante and Beckett?" I raise my eyebrows, wondering if his two other brothers will come.

Theo shakes his head. "You know how Dante is. Won't

even come out of his office to see the sun. He's developing a new security plan for the palace, and he says he's too busy researching. Beckett is away for the month on a trip across Europe."

"You want to do it without them and Luca?"

"It's the solstice," Theo says, as if that explains anything. "I'm sick of tiptoeing around the castle. Ever since Luca's accident, all of Argyle has been in mourning." He snorts, shaking his head. "No one died! Luca is fine. His physical therapy is going well, even if he refuses to talk to us. The doctors think he'll walk again."

I arch my eyebrows. Luca walking again? That would be nothing short of a miracle. If he recovered, would he want to pick up where we left off?

Would *I* want that?

The churning in my gut tells me no, I wouldn't. I'm leaving Argyle next week. I'm doing something for *me*. I'm pursuing my dreams, not falling back into the arms of a man who didn't want me. Maybe he never wanted me.

It's over between Luca and me. Has been for a long, long time. His recovery won't change that.

"Come on, Cara," Theo continues, taking a step toward me. "I'm sick of it. I need to do something fun. Something normal." He takes a deep breath, spreading his palms toward me. When Theo's sharp, blue eyes land on mine, he arches his eyebrows. "I want to hang out with someone I've been friends with for years. Like old times."

"It's not like old times, though, Theo," I say softly.

Something flashes in Theo's eyes. He's always been the quiet one. The dutiful one. But there's a fierceness in his gaze that makes me pause.

He snorts, shaking his head. "What, because Luca had an accident and decided to turn his back on you? On all of us?"

Theo scoffs. "We've been trying to reach out to him ever since he left for Singapore, Cara. *Three. Years.* He thinks he's being some kind of saint for suffering alone, but he doesn't realize how much it hurts for the rest of us. I've seen how much you've been hurting. He's my brother, but he has no right to treat you like that."

The truth in his words makes my eyes prickle with tears. No one has acknowledged how much pain Luca has caused me. My mother tells me I should just try harder to get Luca to come back to me. My father mostly just avoids talking about it.

I know what my parents' unsaid words mean, though: my betrothal fell apart, and it's all my fault.

My mother won't get her 'in' to the royal family. My father's sponsorships and business will continue to falter. Our family will slowly slip out of Argyle's elite, and I have only myself to blame. I didn't do my duty. I couldn't close the deal.

I failed.

So, I'm leaving.

For once in my life, I'm *not* going to do what's expected of me. I'll leave my home and chase my dream. I'll sing every day and pursue something I never thought I'd have. I'll look for adventure. I'll seek out the unknown. I'll have experiences I could never have imagined.

But when Theo stares at me with those crushed velvet eyes, I hesitate.

Our solstice sailing trip is tradition. It wouldn't hurt to do it one last time, would it?

For old time's sake.

I didn't think anyone understood how heartbreaking it's been to watch Luca turn his back on me and be completely powerless to do anything about it.

Theo understands. I can tell by the way he's looking at me

right now. His eyes are asking me to come with him. To sail around the islands and pretend that none of it ever happened.

And one last time, that's exactly what I'll do. This sailing trip will be my final goodbye. My last look at the islands of my home before I leave on my first big adventure.

I try to gulp past a lump in my throat and finally nod. "Okay."

Theo's face breaks into a blinding smile. He crosses the room in three strides and wraps his arms around me, spinning me in a circle. I yelp, clinging onto his broad shoulders. He smells like salty sea air and a fresh summer breeze. His skin is warm under my touch, and it sends a tingle of energy coursing through my hands. When he sets me down, my cheeks are burning.

Prince Theo is the heir to the throne, and although we grew up together, I'm not used to touching him. I was always promised to Luca, and the other brothers kept a respectful distance.

Theo doesn't seem to notice. He slides his sunglasses on and arches his eyebrows. "Ready?"

"Let me get my swimsuit," I say. "Meet you in the car." Excitement curls in the pit of my stomach as a grin tugs at my lips. I slip away from him, rushing up the stairs in my parents' expansive home. Tearing down the hallway, I run to my bedroom. I take a bag out of my closet and start throwing things in it. A spare swimsuit, a change of clothes, a toothbrush, sunscreen—all the things I'll need for a two-night stay on a royal sailboat.

On top of my dresser, my mismatched collection of shells and beach treasures is proudly displayed. I touch each item for good luck. Wrapping my fingers around an old, faded deck of cards with frayed edges, I smile. Then, I slip it into my bag. My heart flutters, and I fly down the stairs again.

The Prince is already waiting in the car outside, but instead of rushing through the front door, I make a hard left and move deeper into the house toward the library.

Rapping my knuckles gently on the doorframe, I wait for my father's deep voice to call out.

"Come in," he says, and I step through the door.

2

———

CARA

MY FATHER IS A TALL, broad man with a shock of shoulder-length white hair. His barrel chest barely fits into shirts, and often he opts not to wear any at all. I've gotten used to seeing the wiry, white chest hair sticking out of his dark skin.

Tristan Shoal doesn't need to wear a shirt. In Argyle, he's the King of the Sea.

He's the only Argylian to ever win an Olympic gold medal. Not only that, but he's the only person—from Argyle or otherwise—to hold the world record for longest unassisted ocean swim.

We used to joke that our family was descended from fish. All of us—my six sisters and I—learned to swim at the same time we learned to walk. My father runs a swimming school here on Argyle's main island and if he's not in the library, he's in the water.

When he sees me, my father stands up. A smile splits his face and he spreads his arms wide.

"Darling daughter," he says, stepping around his desk to wrap his thick swimmer's arms around me. "To what do I owe the honor?"

"Just wanted to let you know that I'm heading out with Prince Theo for the solstice sailing trip."

My father's eyebrows move up a fraction of an inch. The movement isn't lost on me.

"Prince Theo?" he repeats.

I nod. "He's waiting for me outside."

"After everything Luca put you through, you still want to spend time with the royal family?"

I smile sadly, offering the only explanation I have: "It's tradition."

My father sighs, cupping the side of my head with his broad hand. "You're better than them, Cara. No matter what your mother says. Luca never deserved you."

Tears prickle at my eyes.

Why would he say that *now*? After three whole years of torture, he finally tells me what I've been dying to hear?

A lump forms in my throat. I haven't told my father I'm leaving. I haven't even told him I applied to music schools. I got an interview at The Juilliard School, in New York, and I had to pretend to go visit one of our distant cousins just to attend the interview and audition.

I never heard back, so I assumed I didn't get in.

Words don't come. I need to tell him that I'm planning on going, but I don't know how to say it.

I don't know where I'm going, or when I'll be back. I'm leaving the safety of my childhood home to see what else the world has to offer. I have no plan and only a little bit of money.

I know he won't approve.

"It's just a sailing trip, Dad," I finally manage to say. My voice is small, and the lump in my throat grows bigger. "I'll be back in two days."

What I really want to say is, *I'll be back soon. Maybe two weeks. Two months. Two years. Who knows? I need to see what else is out there in the world, without living under the shadow of the King of the Sea. I need to pursue my own dreams, instead of reliving my father's. I need to be someone other than Tristan Shoal's youngest daughter.*

I need to go.

"Be careful," he says. "Respect the ocean."

"I know, Dad," I smile. "You taught me to swim. I'll be okay. I learned from the best."

"Listen to the ship's captain and crew. Don't let the Prince convince you to do anything silly. Not too much drinking, and no swimming if you've had a few drinks. And—"

"Dad!" I interrupt, laughing. "I'll be *fine*."

His brow creases as he lets out a sigh. "I know. I know. I just worry when you leave my sight."

My heart squeezes. He's worried about me going on a sailing trip on the royal yacht, with world-class sailors and all the comforts of the royal family. How will he react when I tell him I'm leaving to explore the world, with no plan and no safety net?

"When you get back, we can talk about the business. Have you given any more thought to taking over the Shoal Swim School? You know I'm getting older and your sisters haven't shown much interest. I want you to step up, Cara."

My heart squeezes. We've talked about this so many times, and he's never accepted my refusal. I let out a sigh and shrug my shoulders. "I don't want to run the school, Dad. I told you this."

"You're the best swimmer in Argyle, apart from me. You grew up in the ocean. There's no one better than you to take over from me, Cara."

"What about one of my sisters? Christine is at least as

good a swimmer as me, and she has a better brain for business."

"It's not about business, Cara." My father smiles. "It's about heart."

"What if my heart isn't in it?" I stop myself from speaking more, wanting to tell him the truth. I want to tell him my heart wants to sing. That I want to leave Argyle and find my own way in the world.

My father smiles softly and wraps me in a tight hug. "Let's talk about it when you get back."

When we pull apart, his eyes are misty. My father is a large man, and I'm not used to seeing him teary-eyed. He clears his throat and nods to the library door.

"Go. Don't leave the Prince waiting."

I slip out through the door as emotion tightens my throat. It's not that I *want* to leave home—I *have* to. I'm compelled, like some hook has dug itself into my gut and is pulling me away. I need to see more of the world and discover things for myself.

I need to get away from the memory of Luca, and all the broken promises that he brought to me.

Will my father understand that, though?

Before I get to the front door, with my swimsuit on under my clothes and my bag slung over my shoulder, my mother appears in front of me.

She's the exact opposite to my father. She's thin and wiry, with sharp, green eyes. Her skin, contrary to my father's, is pale and almost translucent. As always, her lips are painted bright red.

My mother isn't a champion swimmer. She married my father when they were very young, and I think part of her resents the fact that Tristan Shoal is celebrated throughout the Kingdom while she's only seen as his wife. Her family is part of the old aristocracy in Argyle, but their fortunes have been declining.

She had my six sisters and me when she was young, and her whole life has been dedicated to making sure our family is well-taken care of.

I should be grateful for everything she's done. I know I should. It's just that where my father's arms are like a warm, tropical breeze, my mother's embrace is a cold wind whipping through a barren countryside. I'm not supposed to be afraid of my own mother, but deep down, I have to admit she intimidates me.

I've always thought she married my father because she thought he would raise her name back up to its former glory. But my father mostly cares about swimming, and the Shoal Swim School offers far too many scholarships and free programs to turn much of a profit.

When my father wasn't the path to riches for her, my mother arranged to marry my sisters off to dukes and earls, with the final jewel in her crown being me. I was supposed to be a princess.

And I failed.

Ever since Prince Luca left to get surgery on his back, my mother's been in a foul mood. My marriage into the royal family was supposed to secure my whole family's future. Joining with the royal family would ensure that we would never have to worry about a thing—even with six of us daughters and a retired Olympian to provide for.

Then, it all fell apart.

Luca doesn't want me anymore.

"Going somewhere?" my mother asks, arching an eyebrow.

"Sailing around the Kingdom." I try to step around her,

but my mother shifts to block my path. I try not to squirm under her hawk-eye stare.

She glances out through the open door and slides her gaze back to me. "With Prince Theo?"

I nod. "Yeah."

Something flashes in my mother's eyes, and an uncomfortable feeling snakes down my spine. I can almost hear the gears grinding in her head.

Discomfort twists inside me as my stomach clenches. I haven't seen that look on her face since I was a young teenager, and it was decided that Luca and I were perfect for each other. I don't want her to get any ideas right before I leave this place for good.

"Got to go. Bye!" I yell, dodging around her. I rush through the door and slam it behind me.

As soon as I skid to a stop beside the Prince's convertible, he flashes another smile at me and leans over to open the door. I toss my bag into the back seat and slide in. The unease in my heart evaporates.

"Ready?" he asks, grinning.

I nod. "As ready as I'll ever be."

The Prince revs the engine and takes off down our long, winding driveway and out through the estate gates. The convertible roars beneath us as Theo shifts gears. I lift my arms up to feel the rush of the air as we drive, finally letting myself smile in earnest.

It feels like old times. Before the accident. Before Luca went to Singapore. Before he pushed me away.

Like all those years when the Princes and I would spend long, summer days together. When we'd laze on sailboats and go swimming for hours. When we'd come back home with wrinkly fingers and toes, and hair bleached by the sun.

A laugh explodes out of me as the wind whips through

my hair. I glance at Prince Theo, leaning over to rest my head on his shoulder. He slings his arm around me and gives me a nudge, grinning.

"Happy?"

I nod. "Yeah. Happy."

And it's the truth.

I've been excited to leave Argyle. I've been looking forward to making a future for myself, away from my family and my home. I've been looking forward to exploring a new world and trying to make it as a singer.

But have I been happy? Really, truly, throw-your-arms-out-of-a-convertible-and-let-out-a-scream happy?

I can't say I have.

"I knew you would be." The Prince grins, accelerating down the road. "I couldn't go another year without doing this. It's tradition. It's important. The past three years have been a mess, and I think it's time we start enjoying life again."

"Couldn't agree more," I say, my smile splitting my face in half. My cheeks already hurt.

We slow down as we arrive at the royal marina, and Theo's personal sailboat is a hive of activity. Half a dozen members of staff are walking on and off, preparing it for its time at sea. We won't be out there long—just two nights—but the royal preparations leave nothing to chance.

Theo glances at me, smiling. "Did you bring the deck of cards?"

A flash crosses my eyes as I grin. "Yup. Wouldn't be the solstice sailing trip without them."

"Good." The Prince opens the convertible door and strides toward the waiting sailboat. I grab my bag and scamper after him, excitement igniting in the pit of my stomach.

After three years of pain and countless sleepless nights

thinking about Luca, this is the first time I feel like myself again.

It's the perfect way to leave Argyle. I'm not leaving after a year of misery. It's my final tour to the island of my youth, and the last little bit of familiarity before I take off for a new beginning.

As soon as I step onto the royal yacht, my heart feels at ease. Most of the staff members walk off, leaving Prince Theo and me with a chef, the captain, and a two-man crew. Usually, we'd have the other princes here, too.

Theo doesn't seem to mind. He shakes the captain's hand and looks over his shoulder to smile at me. I inhale the sea air, closing my eyes to enjoy the sun's rays on my skin.

After three years of heartbreak, things are turning around. This is the start of the chapter for me. One where I have new experiences and a fresh start.

The Prince is right—our traditions are important. Even if Luca's gone and it's just Theo and me, it matters that we do our solstice sailing trip. It matters that I stay friends with Theo. It matters that we care about each other, even if Luca and I will never be together.

It's one last sailing trip to send me off into the world—the perfect goodbye.

3

———

THEO

"Sing me a song, Cara."

I stare up at the night sky as a thousand stars twinkle down at me. Gentle waves lap at the sides of the sailboat. The sound of the shore has long since faded, and Cara and I are alone on board with the captain, crew, and chef.

Cara groans beside me. I turn my head to see her lying on the yacht's deck beside me, her dark, reddish-brown hair splayed around her head. Big brown eyes stare back at me, and she shakes her head.

"It's bad luck to sing at sea."

"It's bad luck to have women on board, yet here you are."

"Why are there always women carved on the bow of a ship, then?" She arches an eyebrow.

I grin. "They're topless. That makes it okay."

"Bullshit."

"Hey, I don't make the rules. Long John Silver says topless women are okay, and clothed women aren't. Who am I to argue with him?"

Cara laughs, shaking her head. God, I've missed that sound. For most of my childhood, Cara was with us at the castle. Whenever court life became too serious, I could always count on her to cut through it with a laugh.

Where my life has been defined by duty and responsibility, Cara has always been carefree. It's one of the reasons I wanted to take this trip this year. One last time feeling free until I was chained to my title.

She snorts, shaking her head. "I'm not taking my top off, you pervert."

"I only asked you to sing me a song."

She smiles, staring up at the starry sky without answering.

"Come on," I say. "When we were kids, you wouldn't stop singing. Your voice was beautiful."

"I don't want to."

"Why not?" I nudge her, and Cara turns her head to stare back up at the stars. She doesn't start singing, and the only sound is the ocean around us.

Finally, after a long silence, Cara sucks in a deep breath.

"I'm leaving," she says into the night.

"You're what?"

"I'm leaving. Next week, I leave for the United States, then maybe Farcliff, Canada, and who knows? I want to see the world." She glances at me, her bright, wide eyes peering deep into my soul. "I applied to a bunch of music schools, but I haven't gotten into any of them. Most of them didn't bother replying. Could be a blessing in disguise. This way, I can just leave and see where the wind takes me." She lets out a long sigh. "I'm thinking I'll start with Los Angeles. It'll be relatively warm there, so not too much of a shock to my system after growing up in the Caribbean. I'll see if I can get a record deal, or at least make some contacts in the music industry. If not, who knows? I can do something else. I always wanted to be a singer, but maybe I'm just not good enough."

"Bullshit," I answer. My chest is tight. Cara's leaving? For good? First my mother, then Luca, and now Cara, too? I clear my throat. "Your voice is amazing."

"Not according to the dean of admissions for most of the top schools in North America."

"Whatever. Screw them. Sing me something. I'm your future King."

"Playing the King card now, huh?" She grins, shaking her head. "What if I refuse?"

"I'll make you walk the plank. I'll tie you up to the mast and never let you leave."

Cara's laugh rings out in the silent night. "So, life as normal, then. Trapped here to do someone else's bidding."

My eyes prickle and a lump forms in my throat. I wasn't expecting that. It takes me a few seconds to compose myself. "Is this because of Luca?"

She answers with a sigh.

In a way, I'm happy for her. I think Cara deserves to make a new life for herself. She stopped singing around the time she was promised to my brother Luca. It was arranged by our parents, but it still felt natural. They loved each other.

Then, Luca jumped off a cliff and broke his back. He moved to Singapore to get treated, and he pushed us all away. Refused to have us visit. Stopped taking Cara's calls.

I saw her break. We suffered alongside each other, until we drifted apart.

Maybe leaving is a way for her to heal. To find her voice again.

She deserves a fresh start. Cara's always been independent, and I doubt even Luca could have kept her in Argyle for long. They would have had a happy, adventure-filled life together while I stayed at home and ran the Kingdom. I was always a little jealous of Luca—and of Cara, too—but my duty to the Kingdom was more important than any spontaneity.

Now, more than ever, my responsibilities have to take precedence. My father is sick, and I know I'll have to step up soon. In a way, this solstice sailing trip is a goodbye to my youth. I didn't think it would be a goodbye to Cara, too.

"Do you miss him?" she asks in the silence.

I turn to look at her, the moonlight glowing over her smooth skin. Cara doesn't meet my eye. She keeps her gaze on the stars as I stare at her profile.

Has she always been this beautiful? Maybe it's the light of the moon and the gentle rocking of the boat. Maybe it's the two glasses of wine I had with dinner, but Cara seems to have a glow about her that I haven't noticed before. I stare at the curve of her neck and the delicate fullness of her lips, almost forgetting that she asked me a question.

"So... do you miss him?" she repeats softly, staring up at the stars.

"Who, Luca?" I finally answer, the words almost torn from my throat. My brother's name tastes bitter when I say it.

Cara nods without looking at me.

I grunt. "Of course. He's been gone three years. I wish none of this had happened. I wish he hadn't jumped off that cliff. I wish you hadn't been there to see it. I wish everything was back the way it used to be."

Is that true, though? Do I want things back the way they were before? When I'm lying here alone with Cara, I wonder if maybe I don't want things to go back at all.

Silence hangs heavy between us. "How about you? Do you miss him?" I finally ask.

Cara inhales and turns her head to look at me. A soft, warm breeze flows over us, carrying the scent of salty air and seaweed. Her almond-shaped eyes drill into mine as she tucks an arm under her head.

"I missed him desperately for a long time," Cara finally answers. "If he had told me that he wanted to break up with me, I think it would have been easier. But he just pushed me away and forced me to just...give up." She winces, shaking her head. "I shouldn't say that. He broke his back and it was incredibly difficult for him. I wanted to be there for him."

"But he wouldn't let you."

Her eyes meet mine, and the depth of her sadness almost knocks me back. When my brother had his accident, my whole family was in shock. Hell, the whole *Kingdom* was in shock. Luca was airlifted to the hospital in Argyle, and then transferred to Singapore for a series of risky operations to try to stitch his spine back together again.

We tried flying to be with him. We tried calling. We tried talking to him.

He retreated from all of us. He was medicated, in pain, and facing a lifetime without the use of his legs. I tried to understand his reaction, but it was tough to be shut out.

Being here, on the boat with Cara, I realize that she probably suffered more than all of us. They were a couple. She was supposed to marry Luca, and then all of a sudden, she was alone.

"I'm sorry I wasn't there for you," I blurt out.

Cara's eyes widen, as if she's surprised that someone would even think about her feelings. She shakes her head. "Don't be sorry. I'm not yours to worry about."

Isn't she, though? It feels like she should be mine to worry about. I stretch my arm out toward her. "Come here."

She hesitates for a moment, and finally shimmies closer to me. When Cara's head rests on my shoulder, a wave of calm washes over me. The weight of her head on my chest, and the warmth of her body next to mine feels...*right*.

It feels like she's supposed to be there. She fits against me in a way that I didn't even know was possible, like our bodies were made for each other. Two puzzle pieces carved from the same block. An extension of each other.

My body starts to heat up. Warmth starts in the pit of my stomach and slowly snakes its way through my veins. It's an unfamiliar sensation, full of lust and desire. It spreads like a slow burn through my abdomen, making my cock harden and my fingers twitch to explore Cara's body.

But I resist.

It's wrong.

I can't.

We've been friends for years. Since we were kids! She dated my brother from the time she was fifteen until only a couple of years ago. She was going to be my sister-in-law.

I squeeze my eyes shut, trying to ignore the thumping of my heart. Cara's head rests on my shoulder, and she drapes her arm across my chest. Her skin is warm against mine, and all I want to do is trail my hand along her arm, feeling her velvet skin beneath my fingertips.

As she settles into me, the soft noise that slips through her mouth makes my body burn hotter.

Stop it, I tell myself.

I inhale slowly through my nose, trying to ignore the creeping heat spreading through my body. Can she hear my heart racing?

"Come on," I say, shimmying away from her. "Let's play cards."

Mostly, I just need to get Cara away from me. I shouldn't be feeling these things about my brother's ex-girlfriend. We're just friends.

Right?

Cara's lips stretch into a smile. We stand up. The boat rocks gently, throwing her toward me. Cara giggles, catching herself against my chest.

I look down into her eyes, feeling that same stirring of my heart once again.

Clearing my throat, I pull away and nod toward the main cabin. The chef has cleared the table, so it's free for us to play cards.

It's part of our tradition. We don't actually play cards. We build card castles.

Simple, really. The more the boat rocks, the more the cards fall. The more the cards fall, the more you drink. The more you drink, the harder it is to build card castles. And on, and on, and on.

Tradition.

Cara slips into the booth seat at the table and pulls out a deck of cards from her bag. They're the same worn cards that we've used for the past ten years. All three of my brothers, Cara, and I would play card castle games for hours when we were younger. She always had the same deck, ready to pull out of her bag whenever it was needed.

That's one thing I like about Cara. She collects things that mean something to her. They're never expensive things, even though her family is wealthy. The things she collects are usually small, like a worn pack of cards or a couple of nice shells that she finds on the beach. She doesn't value the things that most people in my life hold dear—expensive cars and clothes, jewelry, and money. She values things that have meaning.

Real meaning—like a pack of worn playing cards, frayed edges and all.

Maybe that's why she needs to leave. The things that hold

her in Argyle—stability, safety, a big house that her parents built—don't mean anything to her. She wants to find her own treasures along the way.

I head for the bar and pull out a bottle of whiskey, flashing a grin at her.

"You ready?"

"Ready to win."

The rules are simple. The person that builds the tallest card castle in an allotted amount of time wins. The other person drinks.

We start the first round, and my card castle crumbles as soon as the boat rocks. Cara laughs, nodding to the bottle of alcohol.

"Drink." Her eyes flash.

The alcohol burns on the way down. Cara giggles, and sets the timer on her phone again.

It's a silly game, but we've been playing it for years. Cara's tongue pokes out of her mouth as she tries to steady her hands, starting on the second level of her card castle.

My cards are slipping already. I haven't even been able to get the first two to stand up against each other.

My pathetic structure collapses. "I think you rigged these cards."

"I think you've sucked at this game for years." Cara quips. The buzzer sounds, and her smile widens. "Drink."

I take a swig of whiskey, shaking my head as I wipe my lips on the back of my hand. "You've definitely rigged this."

"In all the years we've been doing this, how many times have you won?" She arches an eyebrow.

We both know the answer to that question: zero. My hands aren't steady, and I just can't get the cards to stack up. Add the rocking of the boat and a few drinks, and I'm completely hopeless.

At least I enjoy whiskey.

I just shake my head and pour some alcohol into her glass. "You should drink for speaking to your Crown Prince in that tone."

"Oh, pulling out the royal card again. I see how it is. You've changed, Theo."

"I'm not above using my title to get what I want."

"And what do you want?" Her eyes darken, and heat flames in my gut.

Instead of answering, I just drink.

Cara laughs, and I realize just how much I've missed that sound. She used to be a fixture at the palace. We grew up together, and I called her one of my closest childhood friends. Things changed when she was promised to Luca, obviously, but we've always been close.

The past three years I've seen less of her than ever before, and I've missed her more than I realized.

She shows me her phone screen, her finger hovering over the timer button. "Are you giving up, or should we go another round?"

"I never give up."

Cara grins. My heart feels easy. I watch her stack her cards higher and higher, and I resign myself to getting very, very drunk with one of my closest friends.

How could I not? It's tradition.

4

———

CARA

I WAKE up with a pounding headache. Even though I won every single round of the card castle game, I still drank my fair share of whiskey with Theo.

I couldn't help it. It's been months—*years*—since I've been able to let loose. It felt like old times, or maybe like the start of my new life. One where I'm free to get drunk if I feel like it, or leave on an international adventure when I want to. One where I chase my own dreams, instead of living the life that's been prescribed for me.

But as my head thumps, I'm almost regretting it.

Almost.

The yacht rocks, and I groan into my pillow. I can hear Prince Theo moving around in the cabin next to mine, and I wonder if he's feeling as groggy as I am. I don't know if it's the hangover or the weather, but the waves feel choppier than they did yesterday.

Shuffling out of my cabin, I emerge at the same time as Theo appears in his doorway. His hair is mussed and his eyes are hazy, but a tiny kernel of warmth flames to life in the pit of my stomach. Has he always been this handsome?

I clear my throat, trying to shake the feeling away.

Maybe I'm still a little drunk.

"How'd you sleep?" the Prince asks, rubbing his palm over his jaw.

"Fine, I guess. I think it was more passing out than sleeping. How much did we drink last night?"

The boat heaves, and Theo stumbles toward me. He catches himself against my doorway, but not before his chest brushes against mine. The heat in my gut expands as I inhale his scent, not even bothered by the hangover that still pounds in my head.

My thighs clench. My heart stutters.

This is bad.

I'm not supposed to feel this way about Theo. It's wrong on so many levels.

I must be lonelier than I thought. Three years without Luca has taken its toll. It's just hormones. That's all.

Right?

"Coffee?" Theo grunts, nodding toward the galley kitchen at the back of the yacht. I nod, following him down the narrow passageway. My eyes drop to his butt, mesmerized by the motion of it as he walks. Glancing away, I curse myself.

I'm definitely still drunk. There's no other explanation. My thoughts aren't my own.

We make it to the kitchen, where Chef Alfred has prepared a full spread for breakfast. The chef, dressed in his crisp white uniform, bows to the Prince and me before offering us a selection of food.

My stomach gurgles violently. I shake my head.

"Just coffee, please."

"As you wish," Alfred says, pouring coffee halfway up the mug. The boat rocks, sending the hot liquid sloshing up the sides of its container.

"Maybe a mug with a lid." He smiles.

I nod gratefully, accepting the travel mug. Theo's already collapsed on one of the banquettes, his hand over his face as he groans.

"Remind me again why we invented that game? This happens every year."

I chuckle, joining him on the long, cushioned bench. "What did you think was going to happen?"

"I was hoping I'd whoop your ass, for once."

"Dreamer."

Prince Theo groans, and I smile into my coffee.

"Maybe we're getting too old to play it," I say with a shrug. "I don't remember being this hungover last time."

Prince Theo's long limbs are stretched over the seat. When he shifts his body on the bench, the edge of his shirt rides up his stomach, exposing a strip of bronzed flesh. My heart thumps and I have to look away.

The coffee is bitter and hot, and it burns on the way down. I focus on the sensation, because at least then I'm not thinking about Prince Theo's body.

Has he always been this attractive?

I've never thought of him as anything other than a childhood friend. When I was dating Luca, Prince Theo was going to be my future brother-in-law. Theo had always been a little more distant than the other Princes. He's the King-in-training, after all. I've always thought of him as a person who puts duty above everything and takes his responsibilities very seriously.

He was never someone I looked at as anything more than my friend and future King. Plus, I was dating his brother. I was in love, or so I thought.

Now, everything's changed. Luca and I aren't together anymore. It's been years since a man has looked at me, let alone spent any time with me. I've been lonely. Alone. Isolated.

My parents have raged and ranted about the dissolution of my engagement to Prince Luca, my mother always cursing me for letting it fall apart. I was supposed to be their ticket into the royal family. I was supposed to be the one to make their fortune more respectable by marrying royalty. Now, that's all over.

My parents don't know it yet, but I'm leaving. It's done.

Except, when my eyes drift over Prince Theo's body, I can't help but enjoy the embers that burn in my veins. Heat feels good after three years of cold isolation. Being next to him makes something spark inside me. Something that's lain dormant for a long time.

Theo feels me staring at his body and opens his eyes. We look at each other for a moment. His gaze is unreadable.

The chef places some bacon on a hot pan, then, and both our heads turn toward the sizzle.

Then, the smell hits.

Closely followed by nausea.

Theo groans, scrambling to his feet as the boat rocks violently to the side. He catches himself against the dining table, and I'm grateful that everything on this yacht is secured to the floor. Theo's body lands inches from mine, splayed across the table. Even after a night of drinking, he still smells like a fresh ocean breeze mixed with manly musk.

How did I never notice that scent before? Or the way it makes my blood burn hotter?

Groaning, the Prince pulls himself off the table and mumbles something about fresh air.

I watch him leave the small room, closing my eyes as I wrap my fingers around my mug of coffee.

I must be drunk. It's the only explanation for what's

happening in my body right now. I've never, *ever* thought of Theo this way. I've never been attracted to him. I've been able to acknowledge his attractiveness, sure, but in an objective kind of way. The way you can acknowledge a celebrity is attractive without actually being turned on by them. He's never made my pulse quicken like he does now.

I need to get a grip.

I sip my coffee, waiting for my heartbeat to slow down.

Theo is off-limits. I used to be promised to his brother. We grew up together.

He's my *friend*.

Nothing more.

And I'm *leaving*, for crying out loud. In a week, I'll be gone. Now is *not* the time to muddy the waters.

Even if I were attracted to him—which I'm not, because I'm sure this'll pass once the alcohol is out of my system—it would be completely inappropriate. Completely out of the question. Completely wrong.

Still, my eyes drift up to the hallway where he disappeared. Something tugs at the pit of my stomach, and I know I need to follow him.

Heaving myself off the booth seat, I catch myself against the wall when the boat rocks again.

"Captain says a storm's coming," Chef Alfred explains, securing all his things under straps and in drawers. He gives me a tight smile. "We might have to spend the day below deck."

"I'll let the Prince know."

The chef bows his head and continues his work. I hand him my empty coffee mug and head down the narrow hallway. As soon as I emerge into the fresh air outside, my headache eases a little. The heat that burned inside me dampens, and relief floods through my body.

I'm not attracted to Theo. My moment of weakness was only the result of three lonely years and a night of heavy drinking.

I should be grateful that I didn't act on any of these feelings last night. It'll pass.

Scanning the yacht's deck, I see Theo near the railing. The captain is beside the mast of the sailboat with one of the crew members, furiously trying to drop the sail down. The sky is dark. The sea is choppy.

There's definitely a storm coming.

"You need any help?" I ask the captain, who's busy gathering the fabric of the sail and winding it around the horizontal boom sticking out from the mast.

"I'm fine!" he calls out, waving me toward the cabins behind me. "You should get back inside."

Theo turns to look at us. When his eyes swing toward me, my breath catches. Darkness swirls in his gaze as it drops down my body, sending heat pooling in the pit of my stomach.

I know one thing for sure—he's never looked at me like *that* before.

My nipples pucker. Is it his gaze causing that, or the cold sea air whipping around my body? My hair flies around my face as the Prince and I stare at each other from opposite sides of the yacht. My feet start moving before I realize what's happening. I'm drawn to him, like he's got a rope wrapped around my waist and he's dragging me closer. Like I belong to him.

My heart pounds against my ribcage.

I ignore the captain's shouts as he tells us to go inside. Wind whistles around my ears as I walk toward Theo, catching myself on any available railing as the boat heaves beneath me. The storm is approaching, but I only have eyes for the Prince.

I'm powerless to do anything but make my way toward him.

Theo's deep, blue eyes darken as he watches me. His grip tightens on the railing behind him as his eyes drop the length of my body again.

I can't take much more of this. I'll either have to act on these urges or walk away from Theo forever.

Walking away forever would be the smart thing to do. Up until twelve hours ago, I'd have said it was the easier thing to do.

Now? I'm not so sure.

When I reach him, the Prince's tongue slides out to lick his lips. Heat spatters across my face as a blush spreads over my cheeks. My insides are burning up.

"We should get inside," he says, his voice a low growl. I feel his voice in the depths of my body, below the howling of the wind. The captain yells something behind us, but I don't listen to a word of it.

My hangover has been stripped away by the wind. The smell of the sea air reminds me of Theo, and my eyes are stuck on his lips.

Does he feel this electricity between us? Has it always been there?

Theo shifts his weight, turning his back on the captain and sliding his gaze out to sea. The waves are getting higher, and the wind is whistling. The ocean is black.

"Looks like it's going to be bad."

Before I can answer, my ears register a panicked shout from the captain. I turn my head in time to see the boom swinging out of the captain's grasp. Part of the sail is still unfurled, and a violent gust of wind has caught it. The other crew member leaps over to grab a rope, halting the swinging of the boom. The two of them shout again, struggling against the wind that threatens to rip the rope out of their grasp.

If the boom swings all the way around, it'll come straight for us. A death trap. A hurtling metal rod, four inches in diameter, swinging at head-level toward the Prince and me.

My heart stops. The captain screams again, letting out a few inches of rope as he stumbles over the deck.

"Theo—" I gasp as the captain trips again, the other sailor struggling to regain control. I let out a sigh as the two of them grasp the rope together and start to reel the boom back in. The captain's face is red with effort as the boat rocks in the waves.

The Prince's eyes are still staring out to sea. Either he hasn't heard the captain's shouts, or he's choosing to ignore them.

Figures.

Another thing about royalty? They're not very good at following instructions.

My heart is still racing. Ever since I stepped outside and felt the power of Theo's gaze, it's been thumping uncomfortably.

This is different, though. I taste danger on my tongue. Electricity dances over my skin. We shouldn't be out here on the deck.

"We should go inside," I scream above the whip of the wind.

"In a minute," Theo replies, leaning against the railing. "Look at the lightning!" A wave splashes against the side of the boat, dousing us both in salty water.

Then, I hear it.

Another scream from the captain.

I don't have to look over my shoulder to hear the panic in

his voice. He doesn't need to say any words for me to know something's very, very wrong.

I don't have time to think. I can almost sense the long, metal boom coming whipping toward the Prince and me. I can feel it swinging toward us without needing to look.

It'll hit the Prince before it hits me. We'll be knocked unconscious, or worse. Tossed out to sea like two rag dolls, flying into the black waters toward our deaths.

At this moment, it doesn't matter that Prince Theo is royalty. It doesn't matter that there are years of history between us, or that forbidden desire has sparked to life inside me overnight.

All that matters is saving the Prince's life.

If that boom swings over to us and hits him over the head, he'll be thrown overboard with his skull cracked open.

I have a fraction of a second. Less.

I need to act.

The long metal boom rushes toward us as the captain lets out another shout, and I do the only thing I can think of. Throwing all my weight into it, I tackle Prince Theo to the ground.

Little old me, Cara Shoal of Argyle, throws my five-foot-four body against Prince Theo's six-plus feet of brawn. I wrap my arms around his thick chest, pinning his arms to his sides. Putting all the weight of my desperation into the hit, I launch myself against him.

He yelps in surprise, falling backward just as the boom whizzes over our heads. It skims the top of my hair as we tumble to the ground, my chest crushing against the Prince's as I land. A wheeze is pushed out of his lungs as pain rockets through my arms.

I'm pinned against him, with my arms stuck underneath his heavy body.

The boat rocks, and we tumble together toward the railing. His body rolls over mine as more panicked shouts sound. The captain screams something. I don't hear a word of it.

The yacht heaves.

Theo and I roll.

The edge is only inches away, and the gap between the railing is too tall. We're both going to go overboard.

5

THEO

I'D BE LYING if I said I'd never imagined my body on top of Cara's. I spent the whole night plagued by sex dreams I had no right to have. Her arms pinned above her head. My lips ravishing hers. My cock buried deep inside her. Her soft, brown skin under my palm as her hands splay across my chest.

This is different, though.

It's not so much wild, passionate sex as much as *let's try not to die.*

The boom swings past our heads with so much velocity I know Cara just saved my life. I don't have time to thank her, though, because I'm thrown onto my back by the rocking of the boat. Our bodies are wrapped around each other and we roll once more, closer and closer to the edge of the yacht.

Another wave tips the boat and I'm able to catch myself on the railing. I cage Cara's body underneath mine before she can slip farther away, straining against the movement of the ocean as our boat is thrown around by the might of the storm.

Captain Withers yells something, finally getting the

murderous boom under control. He locks it in place, leaning against the mast to catch his breath. The other crew member wraps the final bit of the sail around the boom and secures it with ropes.

I suck in a deep breath, dropping my eyes to Cara's face. The terror in her eyes ices my veins. She puts her hands on my chest, shaking her head.

"That was scary."

"Yeah." I'm panting, my chest pressed against Cara's.

I can't deny that her body feels good under mine. My knee scrapes against the rough, non-slip surface of the boat's deck, but I don't mind the pain. It barely registers on my radar as adrenaline still dumps into my veins. Gulping down breaths, I slowly let my muscles relax and I loosen my hold on the railing post beside us.

Cara's hand drifts up to my jaw, and she shakes her head. "That scared me, Theo. I thought you were going overboard."

I don't know what to answer. The yacht rocks underneath us, but I can mostly ignore it now. Another wave crashes on the edge of the boat, soaking us with cold water. It almost sizzles on my heated skin.

Cara's eyes shine as she shakes her head from side to side, sucking her bottom lip between her teeth. My eyes follow the movement, and the adrenaline inside me starts changing to something else. Something hotter. More forbidden.

Desire.

I can feel her heart thumping. Her body pinned beneath mine. Her curves molded into my body. Her hands on my face.

"Sorry for tackling you," she whispers.

"You saved my life."

Cara's lips drop open to answer, but the storm steals her

words away. The boat rocks and my arm slips. I collapse on top of Cara, my head buried in her neck.

Is it wrong that even though there's a storm raging around us, even though I almost died, even though I should be worried about getting inside and staying safe, the only thing I can think about is how good Cara Shoal smells?

"You two okay over there?" the captain calls out, slinging some ropes over a hook on the deck of the boat. I lift my head to look at him, giving him a weak smile and a thumbs up.

Before I can say anything, though, the ocean throws us another monstrous wave. Even the captain is thrown to the side, stumbling over his feet.

I'm not prepared for it.

I roll off Cara toward the edge of the boat. The railing has a huge gap in it, big enough for me to slip through—and that's exactly what I do.

With the violent swell of the waves, the wind whipping around, and the water soaking the deck, I don't stand a chance. I shout, my body sliding through the opening as waves crash below.

I'm dropping straight into the stormy ocean.

I'm going to drown. I already know it.

The last thing I'll see is the terror on Cara's face as I slip away from her, my arms flailing as I try in vain to grab onto one of the slippery metal railings.

Cara screams, the sound piercing my heart like an arrow. Her nails dig into my skin as my arms slip away from her, my legs already falling off the edge of the yacht.

"No!" she shouts, the sound ripped from her throat. I can hear the desperation in her scream. Adrenaline spikes my veins as fear pierces my stomach.

It's too late.

I'm going to die.

I'm going overboard, and the storm will sweep me away. I'm already gone. The Kingdom will mourn me, and I'll never fulfill my duty and purpose of becoming King.

But Cara's arm wraps around my shoulder. I hear a pop, and pain shatters through my shoulder and chest. Agony rips through me as a scream tears through my throat. A thousand daggers stab at my shoulder as the muscles and tendons stretch and tear.

Pain is too kind a word for what's happening in my body. Agony is too gentle. My legs swing as Cara holds onto my injured shoulder, causing another wave of pain to smash into me. Nausea roils in my stomach as my shoulder screams and throbs.

But I'm not in the water.

I'm not drowning.

With my free arm, I'm able to cling onto the railing post. Cara's whimpering in pain, her arms wrapped around me as her nails dig into my skin. She shouts, wrapping her body around another post as she struggles to pull me up.

Pain rockets through my shoulder. I scream.

My grip on the railing weakens, and I slip a fraction of an inch. Cara cries out again, tightening her hold on my injured shoulder.

"Theo," she screams, yelling into the wind.

Then, another set of hands. Rough, sea-hardened hands. Captain Withers pulls me onto the deck, dragging me halfway across its rough surface until the three of us collapse on the floor. Cara crawls over to me as I clutch my dislocated shoulder.

"Get the fuck inside," the captain snaps, dragging himself up to his feet. He looks at my shoulder, registering the injury, but doesn't change his command. "Go."

Captain Withers helps Cara up as I struggle to my feet,

finally listening to his instruction. As soon as we duck inside, I see the captain head toward the navigation center on top of the ship's deck to point the vessel into the waves. As the yacht turns into the waves, the rocking lessens and I'm able to make my way below deck.

We're too far away from shore to make it back, so we'll have to survive the storm out in the open ocean.

As soon as the warmth of the interior hits me, my legs feel like jelly. I lean against the wall, forgetting that my arm is hanging unnaturally from my shoulder. Agony spears through me. I grimace.

Cara puts her arm around my waist and leads me to the back, where Alfred is cleaning up the remains of our uneaten breakfasts. His eyes widen when he sees us, his gaze dropping to my injured shoulder.

"Your Highness…"

"I think it's dislocated," I grunt.

Cara makes a noise, tears filling her eyes. Her lip trembles, but I don't have time to say anything before the chef sits me down.

"This is going to hurt," he warns. Grabbing a wooden spoon from a drawer, he hands it to me and motions to my mouth. "Bite down."

My head is cloudy. I can't think straight. I don't understand what he's telling me, but I do what he says anyway. I put the wooden spoon between my teeth as Cara shields her eyes.

Alfred braces himself against the bench and yanks my arm back into place. It pops back into my shoulder joint with an uncomfortable snap, and for a brief second, I feel like I'm back to normal.

Then, the pain hits.

A wave of nausea rises inside me as a yell is ripped from

my throat. The wooden spoon clatters to the floor as I grip my shoulder, agony making my eyes water. Tears stream down my cheeks as I inhale, clutching my weakened arm to my chest.

I can't think about anything but the pain. Chef Alfred opens one of the cupboards, bracing himself against the movement of the ship. The sea is rough, even with the captain doing his best to weather the storm.

The chef pulls out a first aid kit and removes a sling, fitting it around my shoulder. Then, he cracks an ice pack open and nods to Cara.

"Hold that on his shoulder. I'll get you some pain meds."

Cara sits down beside me, her eyes full of tears as she holds the ice pack to my shoulder. I close my eyes, leaning my head against the back of the cushioned bench as I suck in a breath.

Cara's floral, sweet scent filters through to me, clearing some of the pain from my head.

"I'm sorry," she whispers.

I manage to crack open my eyelids and glance at her. "For what?"

"For doing this to you."

I grimace through the pain in my shoulder, forcing a chuckle. Shaking my head, I lift my good arm up to tuck a strand of hair behind her ear.

"That's twice you've saved me," I answer, staring into her deep, brown eyes. "First the boom, then going overboard."

"And dislocated your shoulder in the process."

"I'll forgive that in exchange for my life." A tired smile stretches over my lips. Cara strokes my cheek, her touch easing some of my pain.

Exhaustion starts to settle into my bones. The adrenaline is wearing off, and I barely have the strength to open my eyes when my chef-turned-medic hands me a few pain pills.

"Off to bed," he commands.

I'm not used to being ordered around by my own staff, but I'm not in any position to argue.

Cara helps me to my feet, wrapping her arm around my waist to help lead me to the royal cabin where I spent the last night dreaming of her.

She fluffs my pillows and supports me as I lie down, smoothing the blankets over me. Deep frown lines are etched into her face.

When she stands up to leave, I catch her hand to stop her.

"Stay." My voice is gruff. I know I have no right to ask that of her, but I can't stop myself. I don't want her to leave.

Cara's eyes widen. In the low light of the cabin, her brown hair throws off deep coppery glints, and I long to wrap my fingers around it. She sucks her lip between her teeth again, and heat floods through my core.

I beg her with my eyes. I need her here. I can't stay stuck in this tiny cabin, with this boat rocking me from side to side, thinking of how I almost lost my life. I can't stay here with nothing but my thoughts, remembering how perfect it felt to have Cara's body underneath mine.

Because even though I almost died, even though she saved my life twice in less than five minutes, all I can think of is how much I'll miss her when she's gone.

"Please," I say, my voice scratching against my throat. I'm not accustomed to asking. I'm not one to beg. People usually hurry to do what I want before I even know I want it.

But I'm begging now.

Cara inhales deeply, and finally relents. I throw the blanket up to let her crawl in beside me, and she snuggles into bed beside me.

My heart thumps as Cara's head rests on my good shoulder. I put my arm around her, holding her close as we both let the yacht rock us from side to side.

She holds the ice pack to my injured shoulder, and I focus on the weight of her arm across my chest.

My limbs feel heavy, and my eyelids droop. I hold Cara's body next to mine, relishing this moment. She might be gone in a few days, but right now, she's here.

Over the next few weeks, everything will change. I'll have more responsibilities as I step up and become King. I'll be fulfilling the duties that I've been preparing to take on my entire life. There will be so much change, but I feel ready for it.

The only thing I'm not ready to deal with is Cara leaving.

As I drift off into exhausted sleep, the last thing I think of is how good it feels to have Cara sleeping by my side.

6

———

CARA

I THINK Prince Theo has a boner. I can see the bulge under the blankets when I wake up to howling wind and rough seas, but I can't be sure. It's dark.

He groans, shifting his weight as he sleeps and pulling me into his chest. I walk my fingers over his pecs as my head stays nestled in the crook of his shoulder, closing my eyes for just a moment.

I know I shouldn't be in bed with him, and I certainly shouldn't be enjoying it as much as this.

It's wrong.

He's only a friend. There's Luca to think about. There are decades of history between us.

But yesterday, we almost died. We're all but alone on board, apart from the crew. What's one night of platonic snuggling after an ordeal like that?

His cock throbs, and I realize 'platonic' might be the wrong word. The way my heart stutters when I see the movement under the sheets tells me that my body isn't thinking this is platonic either.

I inhale, trying to rid my mind of my treacherous thoughts.

Luca and I aren't together anymore, but that doesn't mean I should sleep with his brother. The best thing for me to do is leave Argyle and not look back. Just like I planned.

"You're awake," Theo says in a low voice. I look up to see his slitted, sleepy eyes looking down at me. Theo's arm stays wrapped around my body, his fingers tracing tiny circles over my shoulder.

I nod. "Yeah."

"Storm sounds bad."

I nod again. My mouth is suddenly dry. Every sense is heightened. The Prince is so *close*. Every part of him is near me. I've never been pressed up against him like this. I've never been in bed with him like this. Never even dreamed of it.

Never dreamed I'd like it as much as I do.

Words stay stuck somewhere in my throat. His hand drifts up to my head, and he combs his fingers through my thick hair.

"Thank you," he says quietly. "You saved my life."

"Well, I wasn't going to let you die out there."

His eyes are low. I like the way his fingers drift over my scalp, and how his heartbeat thumps against his ribcage. My own hand drifts over to his collarbone, his neck, his jaw.

When my fingers slip up to touch his lips, the tension in the air crackles.

It's dark in here. Intimate.

Anything could happen.

I can see by the look on his face that Prince Theo isn't opposed to something happening. All it would take is one movement from either of us. One kiss. One touch.

We're standing on a knife's edge, staring at each other.

Waiting for the other to act.

Waiting to see if it's worth the consequences.

What would happen if we were together, I wonder? Would it be a one-time thing? Would it change my plans? Would it change anything?

Or would it just be a kiss? A memory? A mistake?

It would have to be a secret. Wouldn't it? With everything that happened with Luca, being with me would be wholly inappropriate. Scandalous. Frowned upon. Completely out of the question.

Theo has always been the responsible brother. The future King. He wouldn't want anything to mark his name with scandal, especially not a salacious affair. That would be too much like his mother. He would never want to do anything like that with me.

Right?

The Prince shifts his weight, pulling me closer.

"Cara," he whispers. It sounds like my name is a healing balm to him. Like he enjoys saying it. His uninjured hand drifts from my scalp down my spine, sending shivers tumbling through my veins.

When his palm reaches the small of my back, he presses his hand into me. I melt into his body without resistance.

We're both ready to jump. Consequences be damned.

Heat rips through me at the thought of pressing my lips to his. My body begs me to lean into him, to trace his lips with my fingers, to walk my hands down to the bulge under the covers.

It would be easy. It would feel good.

Instead, I pull away. I tuck my chin into my chest and roll away from Prince Theo, swinging my legs off the edge of the bed.

I hear Theo sigh behind me. He doesn't have to say anything for me to know what the sound means.

He wanted it too.

"I should go back to my cabin," I say, not daring to turn around.

"Yeah." His voice is gruff. It tugs at my heart, sending echoes of desire rattling through my body.

"You need anything for your shoulder?"

"I'll be fine."

I nod, finally gathering the courage to glance back at him. Lightning flashes outside, carving out the angles in his face. Hooded, dark eyes stare back at me.

"I hate that you're leaving," he says.

My heart thuds. I gulp. "I have to. For me. For my sanity."

The Prince grimaces. He shifts his gaze to the dark porthole, where nothing is visible except splashes of water and a dark, stormy sky.

"My father's abdicating."

I freeze. "What? When?"

"Within a month." Theo still stares out the window, and I long to reach for him.

"So that means..."

"I'll be King," he finishes.

I curl my fingers on the edge of the bed, feeling the luxurious cotton sheets between my fingers. My mouth is dry, and I'm not sure what to say.

"Why is he stepping down?"

Theo swings his eyes over to me and lets out a heavy sigh. "He's sick. Been hiding it for years now, but it's getting worse."

"Sick?"

"Parkinson's. It's starting to get obvious. People are talking."

"And he wants you to step in?"

Theo nods. "I'll be the first unmarried King to be crowned."

His words ring in my ears, and I'm not sure why. "Is that... Is that allowed?" I whisper, like I'm afraid to say it too loud.

Theo sighs. "No. At least, I don't think so. I've asked Dante to look into it and talk to lawyers about me being an unmarried King. That's why he couldn't come on this trip." He glances at me. "I'm ready for it. This is what I was born to do. I've always known it would happen."

"It's just sooner than you expected."

Theo nods.

I let out a deep breath. "How do you feel about it?"

Theo chuckles bitterly. "I could sense my father getting worse over the past few months. That's why I wanted to do this trip one last time. I'm not sure I'll be able to do it next year. It might be the last trip I'm able to take for myself."

My chest squeezes as sadness wells up inside me.

Everything is changing. I'm leaving. Luca is already gone. Theo will be King.

This trip isn't just a goodbye for me—it's a goodbye for Theo, too. We're both moving on with our lives.

Only Dante and Beckett are just as they were, but Dante never leaves the castle, and Beckett has always kept to himself. Secretly, I think he resents the fact that he's only a half-brother, born of his mother's affair. Even though the royal family pretends it doesn't matter, everyone knows he'll never have any official duties as a Prince.

"Looks like both our lives are about to change." I reach over to place my hand over Theo's. The warmth of his skin sends sparks flying up my arm as an ache grows in the pit of my stomach.

The Prince curls his fingers around mine. My body

screams at me to lean over and press my lips to his. I can tell by the look in his eye that he wants it, too.

But once again, I pull away.

I have to.

He's the future King, and who am I? I'm the girl that was supposed to marry his brother. I'm a wannabe singer who won't be here next week. The daughter of a washed-up Olympian and a social-climbing mother.

A nobody.

He'll probably end up married to some princess from another kingdom, and this night will fade from our memory soon enough.

Pushing myself off the bed, I give Theo a tight smile. "You'll be a great King."

"That's what everyone keeps telling me. See you tomorrow." His eyes speak something else, though. They say, *Stay. Come back. Wrap your legs around me and let me claim you right here in this bed.*

It takes all my willpower to tear myself away from his gaze. Heat pools between my legs as I turn away from the Prince, the echo of his skin still burning against mine. As soon as I exit his room, I lean against the wall and let out a sigh.

Leaving is the right thing to do, but it feels so, so wrong.

Tiptoeing back to my room, I collapse into bed. Even though we're on a boat, the mattress is plush and comfortable. I sink into the pillows, staring up at the ceiling as I squeeze my eyes shut.

Prince Theo and I have no future together. There's no point in pursuing any sort of temporary desire that may exist between us.

Even if I hadn't dated his brother, he's one of my closest childhood friends. He's the next King, and I'm only a commoner. My family may be well-off and well-respected, but I'm not a future queen.

Now, more than ever, Theo is off-limits to me.

I roll onto my side and pull the blankets up to my chin. The boat rolls in the waves, and I try to ignore the cracking of the thunder and the flashes of lightning outside. I force myself to sleep, hoping I won't dream of Theo.

WE DOCK EARLY in the morning. Captain Withers looks haggard and tired, with big blueish-black circles under his eyes. The lines on his face are deep-set, and he nods at me as he helps me off the yacht.

"Thank you for yesterday," I say.

He grunts in response, turning back to the boat as soon as I'm safely off the yacht.

Prince Theo waits for me at the end of the pier. I have my overnight bag slung over my shoulder, and I walk over to stand beside him. We watch the first rays of sun peek over the horizon as dawn breaks, and a shiver courses through his body.

"Guess I'd better get you home." When his gaze swings toward me, it sends a jolt of heat straight down my spine. Regret roars inside me at the thought of what could have happened last night.

My throat is tight. I gulp, nodding. "Yeah."

Theo turns away from me to head back down the pier, and I reach out to grab his hand. He pauses, turning to look at me with unreadable eyes.

"Thank you," I say. "Even with the storm, it was nice to spend time with you again. And... good luck. You'll be a great king."

Prince Theo's lips flatten, and he turns away from me

without answering. Pain pierces through my chest, and I wonder if I've done something wrong.

Maybe I shouldn't have left his bed last night. Maybe I should have stayed and acted on my impulses.

But where would that leave me? What future is there between us? What kind of person does it make me if I jump from one brother to the next?

We drive without speaking. Both of us ride in the back seat, and one of the royal chauffeurs ferries us back toward my parents' house. Theo can't drive with his injured shoulder.

When the car pulls up outside, Theo finally breaks the silence. "Thank you for saving my life."

"Twice," I add.

For the first time all morning, Theo cracks a smile. "Twice."

"Don't be a stranger, okay? I..." I hesitate, and then suck in a breath to gather my courage. "I missed you."

Theo holds my gaze as he nods. "Me too."

Leaving him is hard. It feels final, like even though we spent our childhoods together, even though we had traditions and good times, it's all coming to an end. There's no space in my life for him, and there's no place in his life for me.

I watch the royal vehicle drive away, and then trudge up the wide, slate staircase to the big double doors of my parents' home. When I step inside, I hear voices coming from the library.

My mother and father are arguing.

With drooping shoulders, I try to tiptoe toward the staircase. I don't have the energy to deal with any fights right now. I can't face my mother and her eagle-eyed stare. I can't look at my father's face. Everything feels like a lie when he doesn't know I intend to leave next week.

But as I near the staircase, my parents' words become clearer.

"You should be happy I did this, Tristan," my mother says. "After the ordeal with Prince Luca, we almost lost our chance to be part of the royal family."

"I don't care about being part of the royal family!" my father booms.

I freeze with my foot on the bottom stair.

"You got your Olympic gold medal nearly twenty years ago, Tristan. Your sponsorships have all dried up, and you insist on running that charity for underprivileged swimmers that you call a business. We have seven daughters to take care of! Charity isn't paying the bills. We need something else. Cara is our best hope."

"Six of our daughters are already married. Why can't you just let Cara be? Why does she have to be thrown into a marriage that she doesn't want?"

"She would be lucky if we were able to pull this off. The King seemed receptive, but we have to act fast. I've heard rumors of an abdication. Who knows if he has another woman planned for Theo?"

My blood ices. I creep closer to the voices, hugging the wall as I make my way toward the library.

My mother continues. "Besides, who said she doesn't want it? Theo was here the day before yesterday, and I saw the way he looked at Cara."

"That's how *everyone* looks at Cara, Selma. He loves her because they grew up together, not because he'll agree to *marry* her. You had no right to arrange anything without speaking to me, or her, or Theo himself."

"I haven't arranged anything. I've only planted a seed."

"Well, you have no right to plant seeds without my knowledge."

"Please," my mother scoffs.

Planting seeds? Theo? What are they talking about? My heart thuds as I reach the edge of the doorway. I pause. My back is glued to the wall and I'm almost afraid to take a breath.

What did my mother do? Why is my father so upset?

Their voices drop, and I lean my head off the wall and closer to the doorway. I can only hear snippets of words, and I creep closer to the doorway.

I *need* to know what they're talking about. I need to know what my mother has planned, even if it's just a planted seed.

She's never been supportive of my singing. She's never wanted me to have my own voice or my own life. She just wants me to be some cash cow that she can marry off to the highest bidder.

That's why I haven't told my parents I'm leaving. The more time I give my mother to sabotage my plans, the more chance she has of doing it. I wish I didn't have to do it this way, but I do.

Now, more than ever, I need to leave. Especially if she's planning on arranging another relationship for me.

Just when my head is about to poke through the doorway, my father comes rushing through. I yelp, tumbling backward and falling onto the floor. My father lets out a surprised gasp, scrambling back.

"Cara," he sighs. "It's you."

His face is dark. I stare up at him from my spot on the ground, not sure if he's angry with me or not.

Then, my mother appears in the doorway. A wicked smile curls her lips as she crosses her arms across her chest.

"Well, well, well, speak of the girl herself. If you play your cards right, my darling daughter, you'll have gained yourself a husband."

7

THEO

I ASK my driver to take me straight to the royal doctor. His office is located in one of the outbuildings on the palace grounds. My shoulder is throbbing, and I already know I've done some lasting damage. I need the doctor to run some tests to make sure the injury isn't as bad as it feels.

At least the pain takes my mind off what happened last night.

Or rather, what *didn't* happen.

I almost kissed Cara. Almost did a whole lot more than kiss her, too.

Closing my eyes as the car takes me to the doctor's office, I replay the events of the sailing trip in my mind.

Would it have been so bad if we'd hooked up?

Yes, of course it would have been bad. I'd be betraying my brother, for one. It would be an incredibly irresponsible act, which I can't afford when I'm so close to becoming King.

I've known Cara since we were kids. She's one of the only people outside of my immediate family that has been genuine to me. One of the only people that I can call my friend.

And now, I want to throw that all away just to sleep with her?

She's leaving. I can't complicate things for her right as she's starting a new life for herself. I should be celebrating with her and wishing her the best, not imagining what it would feel like to have my cock buried deep inside her.

Plus, me being King is supposed to unite the Kingdom. I'm supposed to be the fresh, new start for Argyle after a tumultuous time under my father. I'm supposed to turn a new leaf after my mother's affair and exile, not have my own scandal right as the crown is placed on my head.

Sighing, I open my eyes as the car stops. I'm tired. When my chauffeur opens the car door for me, I nod to him and head for the doctor's office. I'm ushered inside and seen to right away.

Perks of being the future King, I guess.

I feel like a robot as I answer the doctor's questions. I explain what happened and how my shoulder was dislocated. I tell him what medication I've already taken, and how the chef put my shoulder back into place.

He orders x-rays and an MRI, and tells me to expect to be in a sling for the foreseeable future.

I just nod and try not to think of Cara.

Her fingers trailing over my lips. Her body pressed up against mine. Her warmth, her scent, her sex. She's burned onto my brain, and I don't know how to get her out.

When I exit the doctor's examination room, my father's butler is waiting for me in the lobby. The old man bows to me.

"Your father would like to see you."

"Now?" I ask, knowing I sound like a whiny child. My shoulder is throbbing and all I want to do is sleep.

The man nods. "Now, Your Highness."

I sigh, gesturing for him to lead the way. When duty calls, I have to answer. I always have.

Even last night, when I let Cara walk away from my bed, I did it because it was the right thing to do. The responsible thing to do. The dutiful thing to do.

Not what I wanted.

We walk across the lush, green lawn and through a garden of succulents and into the palace. The butler leads me to the King's wing of the palace. Taking a small staircase up to the third floor, we make our way to my father's chambers. The butler opens the door for me and bows, closing it again once I step through.

The King, who used to be a force to be reckoned with, is frail. He's in bed, his hands crossed over his lap as he rests his eyes. My father looks like he's aged ten years in the past ten weeks, and it pains me to think he's suffering.

"Theo," he says, opening his eyes and spreading his arms out wide. "Thank you for coming. What happened to your shoulder?"

"We had an incident."

"I hear Cara Shoal saved your life."

"Twice." I echo her words. "News travels fast."

My father grunts. He motions to the armchair next to his bed, his hand shaking as he points. I take a seat, watching him interlace his fingers in front of his chest to stop them shaking. A roguish smile tugs at his lips.

"What?" I ask.

"Well, I think it's very fitting that Cara would save your life. Very consistent with the storyline."

Sighing, I close my eyes. I don't have the energy to deal with my father's riddles. Even when he's frail and sick, he still manages to beat around the bush.

"What are you talking about, Father?"

"Well, about your new fiancée."

The floor bottoms out, and I'm in free fall. Gravity ceases to exist, and I'm unable to move. I sit there with my feet stuck to the floor, ass stuck in my chair, staring at my father. He stares back, waiting for a reaction.

Any reaction.

I'm not giving it to him. I can't. How am I supposed to react? What am I supposed to think?

Cara? My fiancée?

"W-what?" I finally manage.

"Don't look so upset," my father laughs. "She'll be better than your cheating mother was. I made sure to negotiate an infidelity clause."

I shake my head. "No. Absolutely not. I'm not marrying Cara. What about Luca?"

"If you hadn't noticed, your dear little brother seems to have decided he doesn't want to be part of this family anymore. His claim to Cara is no longer valid."

His *claim*? Infidelity clause?

This doesn't sound like a marriage. I know I'm not a normal citizen, but I thought I'd have at least some say in who I married, if I married at all.

"What does Cara have to say about this? When did this happen?"

The world is spinning. I can't marry Cara. What about Luca? Reports from Singapore say he's responding well to treatment, and may even be able to regain his ability to walk. Sure, he pushed her away, but I know my brother. He'll want her back when he's through fighting his own demons.

If he heard about me and Cara...

...it would destroy him. All his progress, gone.

Worse, though, is it would devastate Cara, too. She's about

to start her new life. About to move on. About to chase her dreams.

I would stop all of that for her.

Still, buried deep in the most hidden, dark corner of my mind, a thought sparks to life. Marrying Cara doesn't seem so bad.

If I'm being honest, she's perfect.

She's smart. Has the voice of an angel, even though she doesn't sing much anymore. Her smile lights up a room. She's drop-dead gorgeous, and I can't pretend that I'm not attracted to her.

But I'm not *supposed* to be attracted to her. I'm certainly not supposed to marry her.

My father sighs, shrugging. "I knew it'd take you a while to come around. I didn't commit to the marriage on your behalf."

"Am I supposed to thank you for that?"

"Yes," my father answers simply. "You know you need to marry to ascend to the throne, Theo, and time is running out."

"Why do I need to marry? Have you ever looked into that? Can't I marry later? Or not marry at all?"

"I don't write the laws, Theo. I have to live by them just like everyone else. You should know that as well as anyone. You'll be the guardian of this Kingdom. You must abide by its laws more than anyone else."

I let out a breath, squeezing my eyes shut. My head is throbbing, sending waves of pain radiating through my shoulder. I press my fingers to my temple to try to make sense of what my father is saying.

"So, you arranged a marriage between me and Cara while we were on the yacht?"

"I didn't arrange anything," my father says, waving a

hand. "An opportunity presented itself. Selma Shoal suggested it, and my ears perked up. It would *work*, Theo. It would solve a lot of problems and allow me to step down in peace."

My heart squeezes. I know I need to step up and be King. I know my status as a bachelor is standing in the way of that. I have responsibilities that need to be attended to.

But I can't marry Cara. I'd be asking her to give up her life for me. I'd be telling her not to go on her travels, to stay by my side, to betray Luca.

It's too much to ask.

My father sighs. "Look, Theo, it's a win-win. Tristan Shoal is the people's natural leader. He's the most loved celebrity Argyle has ever had. Marrying his daughter could unite the Kingdom."

I sink deeper into the chair, wincing as my elbow hits the armrest. My shoulder pulses with pain, and I lean my head against the back of the armchair. Everything hurts. I'll have to get more meds from the doctor.

Through my haze of pain, I realize that my father's right. Uniting Argyle will be my hardest task, once I take the throne.

My mother cheated on my father with the King's brother, my uncle, and then ran off with him. Ever since then, the Kingdom has been divided. Half the citizens think my father drove her out of her home and that he should have shown mercy. The other half of Argylians side with the King, and think the Queen should have been punished with more than mere exile.

And my brothers and me? We're stuck in the middle. I'm next in line to inherit a divided throne.

Tristan Shoal, on the other hand, is loved by everyone in Argyle. He holds the only Olympic gold medal Argyle has ever earned, and has dozens of world records for his swimming exploits. The day that he earned the world record for longest unassisted open-ocean swim is a national holiday in Argyle every year.

My father is right. He'd be the people's King, if they had a choice. His daughters are the jewels in his crown. Cara, the youngest and most beautiful, would be the natural choice even if the other daughters were still available.

As much as I hate to admit it, marrying Cara *would* help unite the Kingdom. It would make the start of my rule a lot smoother.

But it would kill my brother. It wouldn't be easy for Cara, either.

The King shifts in bed with a grunt, pushing himself off his pillows. His movements are becoming more labored, and I think he's in more pain than he lets on. He nods to me, his eyes dark.

"You'll get used to the idea. You could do worse."

"Let me think about it," I say, pushing myself to my feet. My shoulder aches every time I move.

"Don't take too long. This needs to be done." The King lets out a heavy sigh. His lips pinch, and the weariness in his face is plainly apparent.

He's suffering. He needs to step down.

Which means I either need to marry Cara, or find a legal reason not to.

"Father…"

"This is your duty, Theo. You have to take the throne, and you have to take a wife. I've done my best to make it easy for you. Now return the favor."

My father levels me with a stare, and I know I can't protest. With our Kingdom already divided, if the people learned of his condition, it would only weaken our position. Argyle needs a strong leader.

Me.

And I need to know if I can ascend to the throne as a single man legally, or if I need to find myself a queen.

"Call Flanders back in here," my father says, nodding to the door behind which his butler disappeared. "I'm ready for my dinner."

I bow to my father, then head out the door. Flanders heads inside the King's bedroom behind me, and I turn down the hallway to find my brother Dante. Winding through the hallways, I make my way to the office at the back of the palace where Dante spends most of his time.

When I enter, the lights are low and half a dozen monitors are blinking with spreadsheets and documents I don't understand. Dante swivels around in his chair, flashing a smile at me.

"Big brother." He grins. "I was wondering how long it would take you to come see me."

"Tell me you have good news."

"Well, my arms are still attached to my body, unlike you." He nods to my sling. "Cara saved you, huh?"

"Twice."

"Badass."

I grunt, leaning on his desk. My head hurts, and I don't know if Dante knows about Father's plan to marry me to Cara.

"So? What have you found about the marriage issue?"

Dante lets out a sigh. His smile fades. "Haven't made much progress. I've engaged an independent lawyer to look into it. I trust him," he adds. "But it'll take time to figure it out. The legal texts we have to look through are over a hundred years old and a lot of them only exist in the Royal Archives."

"I don't have time." I rub my forehead and then look at my brother, sighing. I explain to him the conversation I just had with our father, and how time is running out.

Dante rubs his jaw with his hand and turns back to his multitude of computer screens. "I need at least two weeks, Theo. Can you do that?"

"Two weeks?"

Dante nods. "Delay. Tell Father you'll think about it, that you need to get to know Cara or something. Make up some bullshit he'll believe about true love and compatibility."

I scoff, and nod. "He doesn't believe in love."

"I'm not so sure," Dante shrugs.

"I'm going on a pre-coronation tour of the islands for three weeks starting the day after tomorrow," I say. "I could ask him to wait until after that, but who knows what he'd do while I was away."

Dante taps his chin as he thinks. He glances at me, arching an eyebrow. "What if you bring Cara? Then no one can pressure her while you're gone. You know how Father is once he gets an idea. He could have the whole thing organized while you're away, but not if neither of you are here."

I chew my lip. It's not a bad idea. Cara is supposed to leave, but maybe it would be better if she was with me. If our parents are plotting to push us together, we might be able to pretend to play along for a bit. It would give me some time to figure things out and would protect Cara from any unnecessary pressure from her family—and mine.

"I'll see what I can do."

"Good luck." Dante stares at his screens as he taps something on a keyboard. I retreat from the room, rounding my shoulders as I trudge up to my chambers.

As the thoughts swirl around my head, I have to admit something to myself. Something buried deep in my heart, in a hidden corner that hasn't seen the light of day in a long, long time.

Marrying Cara excites me.

I can pretend that I don't want to do it. That I feel bad about betraying my brother. That it's wrong to marry her. Something has shifted inside me, and Cara isn't off-limits anymore.

The simple truth is, I want her. Badly.

8

—————

CARA

"FROM LITTLE OLD Cara Shoal to a Queen," my sister Christine titters, spinning circles around me. "I can hardly believe it."

"It's not right."

"Oh, come on," our eldest sister, Cathy, sighs. "Mother did well to get you that match. I had to marry boring old Count Yara."

"I'm not marrying anyone, and I'm not going to be Queen." I sigh, kicking my feet in the sand as my sisters and I walk down the beach.

"What, you thought that the rest of us would carry the burden of caring for our family? We all had to do things we didn't want to do. Going off to singing school wasn't going to help mother and father provide for our family." Cathy, ever the pragmatist, arches an eyebrow at me.

"But *why*? Why did we have to marry well? Who cares? It's not like we're royalty. Father's an ex-Olympian. Mother is a smart businesswoman. Why couldn't we just do whatever we wanted with our lives? We don't need a house that big. We don't need to live like the royal family. Why can't we just be *normal?*"

Why can't I just leave this place behind and pursue my own dreams?

"That's not how it works, Cara," Christine says, nudging my shoulder with hers. She smiles sadly.

Waves crash on the shore as seagulls squawk above us. The sun dips lower, and soon it'll be touching the horizon. It's been over twelve hours since I left Theo's company this morning, but I haven't stopped thinking about him for a minute.

My future King. If my mother gets her way, my future husband.

I can't wrap my head around it.

If betraying Luca didn't kill me, giving up my dreams when they're almost within reach surely would. I'm *leaving.* I've already decided. Even if my mother plots and conspires until she's blue in the face, I won't marry someone I don't want to marry.

I'm not going to be Queen.

I'm not going to betray Luca.

I'm not going to give up all my dreams in order to marry a man that I never saw as anything but a friend...

...until last night.

Why am I so against this marriage? It's not because I don't want Theo. If the solstice sailing trip was any indication, I'm more attracted to the Crown Prince than anyone, ever.

My mind keeps circling back to Luca. Sure, we broke up. Yes, he shattered my heart. He pushed me away for months until I felt like a shell of who I used to be.

But to marry his very own brother?

That's low. That's not something I ever thought I'd do.

"What about Luca?" I ask my sisters.

Christine picks up a long piece of seaweed and flings it toward the ocean. "What about him? He left you and refused to let you see him. He ignored you for months. You waited for him long enough, Cara. If you ask me, he deserves any pain that comes to him. He treated you badly, even though you'll never admit it. You dedicated your life to being his future wife, for what? To be tossed aside when you begged him to let you help?"

"But to marry his brother? Isn't that wrong?"

"What's wrong is for Luca to think that he can treat you like dirt and then have you wait for him. It's been three whole *years*, Cara. He hasn't called you even once. You went to that silly P.O. box every single day hoping he'd write you. You should've seen the disappointment on your face every time you opened it up to see it empty. I watched you break, day by day. You shouldn't care about him. Luca doesn't want you."

A few months ago, her words would have torn me to shreds.

Now?

Surprisingly, they don't hurt at all. I think that I might have moved on from Luca, but that doesn't mean I'm ready to marry his brother.

The three of us head back toward my parents' house, where I'm sure the chefs will have prepared a lavish meal for us.

My gut twists. I don't want any of it.

I want to *leave*. I want to start fresh. I don't want to hurt Luca, even if he did hurt me. I don't want to marry Theo. I want things to be easy and clean.

Even if I'm not good enough to get into singing school, I still want to see what else the world has to offer. My dreams of becoming a decorated, educated singer might never happen. But who knows? Maybe I could still find a way to make music part of my life.

One thing I know for sure is it's not going to happen if I stay here and marry Prince Theo.

"Well, well, well," Cathy chuckles darkly, pulling me from my thoughts. "Do we think this is a coincidence?" She jabs her thumb down the side of the house, where a familiar black royal vehicle is parked.

Prince Theo.

Christine titters, throwing her dark, curly hair up into a ponytail. She grins at me, shaking her head. "He's come here to claim his bride."

"Oh, please."

"When was the last time the Crown Prince came to our house for Sunday dinner? Oh, right. Never. Not even Luca came here. Prince Theo is here for you." Cathy throws me a glance, shaking her head.

My pulse quickens as we slip in through the side door. I hear voices down the hallway, and nod to my sisters.

"You go ahead. I'll be right there."

Cathy arches an eyebrow but says nothing. The two of them continue down the hall as I duck into the bathroom.

Locking the door, I lean against the vanity and close my eyes.

My mind and body are at war.

The independent, adventurous side of me is screaming to refuse the engagement. Leave Argyle. Go sing in a dirty dive bar for a few bucks. Explore the world.

The impulsive, carnal side of me wants to stay. See what Prince Theo *really* has to offer.

I comb my fingers through my hair and re-adjust my clothing. I can do this. I can stick to my guns. I'll walk out the door and find Prince Theo. I'll tell him I can't do it. I'll say I have to leave. I'll refuse him.

Inhaling, I turn the doorknob and step out. As it turns out, I don't have to go far to find the Prince. He's standing right outside the door.

"Hey." He stares at me in all his brooding glory.

I jump, startled.

"Sorry." The Prince roughs his fingers through his hair. His other arm is still in a sling. My eyes drop to the little strip of skin that is exposed between his trousers and his shirt when he lifts his arm. A deep, muscular V is carved into his lower abdominal muscles, and my mouth starts to water.

Is it wrong that I'd love to trail my tongue right down that muscular groove?

Yes. Wrong. Bad Cara.

Theo smiles at me, and that's all it takes for heat to spark between my thighs. I clench them together as a blush creeps over my cheeks.

It feels like a switch has been flipped inside me. Theo went from being a friend, to all of a sudden being the one man that manages to make me melt with nothing more than a glance.

Whether it's the knowledge that he's the future King—and my potential husband—or just some innate quality of the ultra-good-looking, all of a sudden, it's hard for me not to twirl my fingers in my hair and bat my eyelashes whenever he's near.

I'd be embarrassed if I had enough extra brain cells to use on embarrassment. Right now, they're all occupied thinking of all the compromising positions that the Prince has had me in over the past twenty-four hours. None of which ended the way my body had hoped.

"Your Highness," I say, nodding. "Didn't think I'd see you here tonight. To what do we owe the honor?"

"You know why I'm here, Cara." His voice is gruff, his eyes low.

Why is that so hot? His scratchy voice. His dark eyes. Everything makes me want him. Shouldn't I be telling him all the reasons I can't marry him?

"Yeah," I manage to croak.

"My father told me about the proposal today. I'm sorry they sprang it on you without warning. I didn't know either, if that makes it any better."

"So you..." I clear my throat. "You want this?" I move my finger between the two of us.

He swallows, and I watch his Adam's apple bob up and down. "Uh... Do you?"

"I... I can't." My voice is small. It's hard to say the words. I stare up at him, blinking rapidly. "I have to leave, Theo. Everything I told you on the sailboat is still true. I have to see the world for myself. Get out of here. Move on."

Theo sighs, nodding. He tilts his head back, staring at the ceiling. "Then I have a favor to ask."

My heart thumps. "Uh huh?"

"I need you to pretend." His eyes land on mine, sending another wave of heat coursing through my veins. How does he do that with nothing but a look?

Then, my brain processes his words, and I choke on my own spittle. I cough, hitting my chest with my hand before looking at him. "Pretend?"

"I know it sounds crazy. Dante needs a couple of weeks to talk to lawyers and figure out if I actually need to marry to take the throne. I was thinking..." He trails off, biting his lip.

"What?"

"I have a tour of the islands coming up the day after

tomorrow. It's three weeks long. It might be better if you come with me."

"How would that be better? Won't that be sending a message to our families and the Kingdom that we're going to be married?"

Theo sighs. "I'm worried that if you're here and I'm away, there might be more pressure on you. They might threaten you, or make you agree to things without my knowledge. If you fight it, they'll fight harder. At least if we're both gone and both together, it'll keep them happy for a while. It'll buy me some time."

"So we pretend to agree."

Theo nods. "Or at least, we pretend to consider it." His brows are drawn together, concern etched on his face. "I know. I'm not asking you to give up your dreams, Cara. I just need time."

I gulp. My thoughts are at war with each other. I was supposed to leave the Kingdom this week and start my new life. I was supposed to chase my dreams. Now, the future King is asking me to stay and pretend to be his future fiancée.

The Prince sighs, taking a step closer to me. He strokes the side of my cheek with his good hand and I close my eyes, leaning into his touch.

How does he manage to smell so good all the time? Being near him is like standing in a soft ocean breeze on a warm day.

When I open my eyes again, Theo's chest is almost brushing mine. His eyes are low. When his tongue slides out to lick his lips, my heart stutters.

"I guess I could delay my disappearance," I say in a small voice. A hint of a smile twitches over my lips. "You've been good to me and my family. The least I can do is return the favor."

"You'll get a free trip around the Kingdom, too."

My smile widens. "Could be worse."

The air between us crackles. There are so many things unsaid between us. I can see, reflected in his eyes, the desire I feel. Pretending to be his future fiancée isn't a terrible thought. A part of me kind of likes it.

The Prince lets out a low groan. His fingers stroke my face as he gently shakes his head. "Something happened between us on that boat, Cara."

My throat tightens. I know what he's talking about, but I ignore it. "Uh, yeah. I saved your life." I force a smile. "Twice."

The Prince's hand sweeps along my jaw to tangle into my hair. His touch sends shivers running through my body. Goosebumps erupt all over my skin and I suck in a deep breath to try to contain myself. My fingers disobey, though. They hook into the waistband of his pants and before I know it, I'm pulling him toward me.

The air between us thickens.

A few inches of space separate his lips from mine.

He's right. Of course he's right.

Something happened on his sailboat, and it wasn't me saving his life. It was a shift in the energy that flows between us. A change in the course of our destinies.

This whole marriage thing isn't the cause of it. What's going on between us had already started before my mother decided to find me a royal husband. It started the instant he stepped into my house and asked me to come sailing with him.

The Prince sweeps his thumb over my cheek as he erases the distance between us. My back presses against the wall as his big body cages my much smaller one. I can feel the heat of his chest against mine. The raw power coiled in his muscles.

I want him. Badly.

"There's only one thing that worries me about this plan." His eyes drop momentarily to my lips.

"What's that?" I'm breathless. My body is burning up. My nipples pebble under my thin shirt, and I know the Prince can feel them.

"Whatever's going on between us. That worries me."

The words send a thrill through the pit of my stomach. I like the sound of something going on between us. The more I think about it, the more I like it.

I suck in a breath. "There's nothing between us," I force myself to say.

"No?"

I shake my head. "Nothing."

"Why does that sound like a lie?"

"Because it is one." My voice is a whisper.

Theo grunts. His eyes are hooded. My body screams.

"This is a bad idea, Theo."

The Prince inhales. "I need time. Just for this three-week tour. We can tell your parents and my father that we need to get to know each other."

"We've known each other our whole lives."

"Not like this." His finger strokes my cheek, and a wave of heat crashes into me.

No, definitely not like this.

"Why me?" My voice is a breath. A whisper.

He shrugs, a grin tugging at the corner of his lips. "Could be worse."

"Okay, Casanova." I roll my eyes and shove his chest ever so slightly, clinging onto anything that will cut the tension between us.

What does *pretending* mean right now? I'm not even sure anymore. It feels pretty real to me.

Theo's eyes flash, then, and he angles his head toward me. His lips hover over mine and the heat of his breath sends another wave of electricity tripping down my spine.

"You're special, Cara. More than you know. More than I've let myself admit."

My fingers curl into the waistband of his pants. His skin is hot against my knuckles. His smell is all around me. His lips taunting. My doubts and hesitations get quieter, and quieter, and quieter. 'Pretending' is starting to sound like a good idea. Like the only thing that makes sense right now.

The Prince stares into my eyes. "So, let's pretend to consider the engagement. You come with me on a tour of the islands. We tell no one about the engagement. We tell our parents the only way we'll agree is if we have time to talk it over. Just the two of us."

"Then what?"

"Well, either Dante tells me I can be King as a single man, and you go off on your soul-searching adventure"—his eyes darken as his voice grows hoarse—"or, we decide that we can't live without each other, and you marry me. We live a happy life together and have lots of little heirs."

His words are deliciously wrong. Forbidden. Out of the question.

So why do they sound so good?

I arch my back, pressing my hips against his. It's all the sign he needs.

In the hallway of my parent's house, after aching and wanting and dreaming of him for days, Prince Theo finally, *finally* kisses me. It's more than a kiss. He crushes his lips to mine, pulling my body to him. He claims me with his lips, and I know that I'm already his.

I could deny it. I could pretend I don't want it. I could say that I still want to run away from Argyle.

I'd be lying.

I need his kiss like I need air. When he lashes his tongue against mine, I melt into his embrace. A moan slips through my lips as his fingers curl into the nape of my neck. Needles of pain erupt over my scalp as he tugs at my hair, transforming into pleasure in an instant.

His leg kicks mine apart, and I relish the feeling of grinding myself against him. Every bit of my body is hot. I wrap my arms around his neck and pull him closer as the Prince kisses me harder. He slips his hand under my shirt and sweeps his palms across my back.

His injured arm is pinned between us, pressing up against my body as we moan together.

"Cara," he mumbles into my lips. I love the way my name sounds coming from his mouth. I want him to say it over and over again. I want to hear it as a groan when he drives himself inside me. I want to hear him whisper it in my ear and scream it.

I want Prince Theo. There's no denying it, and no going back. I'm not pretending right now. This is very, very real.

Something changed on that sailboat, and I'm not sure I'm strong enough to resist.

A noise down the hall makes us pull apart. I glance down the empty hallway, then wipe my mouth, stealing a glance at the Prince.

I chuckle awkwardly, smoothing my hair. "Well. That happened."

Theo's lips curl into a grin. He tucks a strand of hair behind my ear and shakes his head.

"Three weeks is all I'm asking, Cara."

"We shouldn't be kissing," I say, even though my lips want more.

"Why not?"

"Because it'll complicate things."

Theo's body is still brushing against mine, and sparks fly between us. He shrugs. "What if I like kissing you?"

"It doesn't change the fact that we're supposed to be pretending. We're not supposed to actually go through with it."

He takes a step back, nodding. "Maybe you're right. We should keep it platonic."

Yeah, right. Whatever that means.

Every time we speak something out loud, our bodies say something entirely different. I want him badly. I don't want to pretend at all. Every single cell in my body wants to go on this tour with Theo, if only to be near him. The voice in my mind screaming that it's a bad idea is too easy to ignore.

But as he takes another step back, I feel the distance between us in my gut, immediately regretting my words. Is it right to push him away? Should I be jumping in his arms?

It feels good, but is it *right*?

I glance at the Prince, who seems to be going through the same turmoil I am. In a whisper, I say the question that keeps plaguing my mind. "What about Luca?"

"What *about* Luca?"

"You know what I mean."

"All I know is my brother lost his chance with you when he pushed you away. You don't have to marry me, but I don't want you to keep torturing yourself over my brother's mistreatment of you."

I chew my lip. Gathering my courage, I force myself to drag my gaze up to Theo's. "Is this a bad idea? Pretending to consider this engagement? We just kissed, Theo. And I'm going to leave when we get back. You're going to be King. It's too complicated. It's a disaster waiting to happen."

Theo lets out a breath. His eyes are clear, and after a

pause, he just shrugs. "Maybe it's best that you're leaving afterwards. Whatever happens between us, we know there's an end date."

I nod, gulping.

The Prince sighs. "I'd be lying if I said I didn't want you, Cara. Whatever happened on that sailboat, it hit me hard. But no matter how much I want you for myself, I don't want you to give up your dreams for me. So, it might seem complicated, but it's really not. I just need your help. No strings attached."

I wish those words didn't have an effect on me. I pride myself on being adventurous. Independent. Thrill-seeking. But having a future King tell me that he wants *me*?

That does something to me.

And it does something to my panties, too.

This is a Bad Idea, with a capital 'B' and a capital 'I.' He might think it's no strings attached—that I'm just buying him time and doing him a favor—but I know the truth. My heart-strings are already tangled. I'm already confused.

I already want him, too.

"Can't you find some other girl, if any woman will do to buy you time? Someone more noble?"

"I don't want someone more noble. I want you."

There it is again. That declaration.

Theo arches an eyebrow, running his thumb over his lip. I follow the movement, my thoughts flicking back to the kiss we just shared.

I nod. "Okay. Just for the tour."

The Prince nods. "Yeah. Just for the tour."

"We don't let our parents push us into this. I still get to leave and chase my dreams on my own."

"Exactly," Theo says, stepping toward me. "I may only be the Prince, but I still won't let my father dictate everything to me, least of all who I choose to marry."

I nod. "Yeah," I agree, even though I'm not sure exactly what I'm agreeing to.

Theo ducks his head down and presses a soft kiss to my lips. Heat ignites in my core again, and I know that things definitely won't be as simple as he claims.

9

THEO

WALKING BACK TO THE SHOALS' living room, my heart is thumping and my palms are sweaty. I know that this plan has the potential to blow up in both our faces in a spectacular fashion. I know that this could backfire. I know that things could go wrong.

But I don't have a choice. I need time to figure this out.

The only way I can think of to keep my father happy and give Dante some time is to tell my father I'm considering this engagement. The only way to keep Cara away from external pressure about this engagement and to safeguard her plans to leave Argyle is to take her with me.

Cara leans over toward me, nudging me with her elbow. "That's three times I've saved your life."

I grin. "At least this time didn't include a dislocated shoulder. Being saved by you is dangerous."

"Careful, Your Highness," Cara grins. The glance she throws my way is indecipherable. I can't tell if she's worried about what we've agreed to do or excited about it.

One thing I do know is my pulse quickens whenever she's around. From the moment things shifted between us on the sailboat, I haven't been able to stop thinking about all the things I want to do to her.

As we walk into the living room, all eyes turn to us. Cara's parents and sisters stare at us expectantly. Cara stiffens beside me, and I can almost sense the regret flowing off her.

I clear my throat. "Thank you for having me. I have to get back to the palace, but I'd like to ask your permission to take Cara on a royal tour that leaves the day after tomorrow."

Mrs. Shoal lets out a squeal, her eyes flashing with a gleam I'm not sure I like. "A tour?" she asks. "That sounds important. You don't need our permission, Your Highness."

"It is important," I answer. "Cara and I have a lot to discuss." The back of my hand brushes Cara's. Heat flows through my arm. My body is far too receptive to her.

No strings attached? Don't make me laugh.

"The Prince and I are just spending time together after a long year apart, Mother. Don't get any ideas," Cara says. Her voice sounds strangled. "We just need to talk everything through."

Mrs. Shoal waves a hand, dismissing Cara's words. The movement doesn't sit well with me, and I know why Cara feels like she has to leave. Being here is stifling.

I steal a glance at Cara. Her face is dark. I can tell she's uncomfortable with this, and she doesn't like lying to her family. Sensing my gaze, she glances up to meet my eye.

"I'll walk you back to your car."

We bid her family goodbye and walk in silence toward the front door. Conflict swirls inside me. On the one hand, the thought of being near Cara excites me. On the other, I know our situation is complicated. I'm asking a lot of her, and not providing much in return.

When we get to my car, my driver hops out to open the back door for me. I stare at the vehicle before turning to face

Cara. Taking her hand in mine, I bring it up to my lips. Her eyes follow the movement.

The memory of our kiss floods my brain. All I can think about is how good she tasted. How right it felt to have her in my arms. How much I wish I had the use of both limbs to wrap around her and never let go.

"So, this royal tour…" Cara arches an eyebrow. "What's it all about?"

"It's a tour of the islands. Three weeks. We'll stop at all the major towns and do a lot of hand-waving and baby-kissing and smiling for the cameras."

"Won't it send a very clear image if I'm there beside you? I thought we were keeping things private. If we start doing a lot of public appearances together, people will talk."

"If we don't spend any time together at all, our families will only put more pressure on us." I take a step toward her, tucking a strand of hair behind her ear. "Please, Cara. I need my father to believe this."

She sucks in a breath, finally nodding. "Okay."

"We leave the day after tomorrow. I'll have the car pick you up."

I almost lean in to kiss Cara again, but hold back. She takes a step away from me, lifting her arm in goodbye.

"See you then."

The royal sea plane is ready and waiting when Cara arrives at the pier. She's dressed in a white sundress, with her long, brown hair trailing down to her mid-back. Against the crisp white of her dress, her skin almost glows. Her lips curl up into a smile and she raises her arm to wave at me. She looks ethereal and regal and completely perfect.

Too perfect.

My body responds instantly, and I have to do my best to keep the fire in my veins under control.

"I couldn't sleep last night," she says, leaning in to kiss me on the cheek. A zip of heat travels down my spine.

"No?"

Cara shakes her head. "Too excited."

"About this trip?"

"Don't let it go to your head," she laughs. "I've never seen most of the islands of Argyle. It'll be my first time on a sea plane. Oh, and I guess you're all right, too."

"I'm flattered." I grin, loving the way her eyes sparkle when she stares at me. "Don't make me feel too special."

"You have an army of people whose job it is to do that," she quips. "I'm not going to be one of them." She grins, squeezing my forearm with her hand before shaking her head. As her face grows more serious, she stares into my eyes. "Thanks for inviting me. I think I need some time away from my mother. She's far too excited about this prospective engagement, but I think you were right to invite me on this tour. It would be tough to leave Argyle now, when all the attention is on me. At least now the attention is on our relationship instead."

I shouldn't like hearing her talk about *our relationship*. It shouldn't send a flow of heat through my chest. It shouldn't make my heart thump at the thought of being near her.

We're not in a relationship. We're only pretending...

...but it feels a little too real already.

The pilot steps out of the plane and bows before helping us inside. He points to two headsets hanging on the plane's walls. "Wear these. It gets loud once I turn the engine on."

Attendants load our suitcases up into the plane, and Cara and I slip the headsets over our ears. The pilot climbs back into the tiny sea plane and starts the engine. It roars to life, and Cara moves a bit closer to me.

I like having her at my side.

Before the plane moves, the pilot speaks into our headsets to give us a short safety briefing while his co-pilot does the last few pre-flight checks. Cara slips her hand into mine, flashing a smile at me after clicking her seatbelt into place.

Then, we take off. The plane skims the surface of the water as the engines roar loud in our ears, even with the big noise-cancelling headsets on. The plane dips from side to side ever so slightly, carving through the surface of the water as we pick up speed.

Then, we take off.

Over the deafening noise of the engines, I can't hear any of the sounds Cara's making, but I can feel her body next to mine. She tenses as we take off, relaxing as the sea plane leaves the surface of the water. We gain altitude and I watch Cara's face turn rapt as she stares out the windows at the water below.

Yachts dot the harbor, and speedboats leave long wakes carved out in the teal water. As we fly higher and higher, Cara laughs and points out islands, sandbars, and flocks of sea birds below us. At the low altitude of the plane, we can see everything.

I mostly watch Cara, though.

I've spent the last year worrying about my father, about my brothers, about my future as King of this nation. Everything has been focused on responsibilities. On duty. On my work in service to the Kingdom.

Now, mostly alone in this sea plane with Cara, seeing the entranced expression on her face as she looks at the scene below, I feel happy. Calm. Free.

I'm not the Crown Prince with the weight of the Kingdom

on my shoulders. I'm not protecting my father's reputation and news of his illness from the public. I'm not worried about whether or not my brother Luca will walk again. I'm not waiting for news on the legality of my ascension to the throne, or wondering if I'll want to marry Cara for real.

I'm just sitting in a sea plane beside a beautiful woman, smiling as we watch the islands pass below us. Cara's hand stays curled around mine, and she moves closer to me. Her body molds against me as she leans over to point something out.

I nod, pretending to look where she's gesturing. My eyes always slide back to her, though. Her eyes, rich and brown and expressive. Her neck, long and graceful. Her lips, full and kissable.

Everything about her is perfect.

In that moment, flying above the Kingdom that will soon be mine, I know that I don't want to pretend at all.

10

CARA

WHEN THE SEA PLANE LANDS, I squeeze Theo's hand so hard I think I might break his fingers. Wouldn't that be a great start to a fake engagement? Injuring both his arms in less than a week?

I can't help it. This plane is tiny, and even though the pilot and his co-pilot are professionals, I feel every wave as we land, every gust of wind, every bump and shake.

But we do land, and the pilot cuts the engines to a dull hum as we taxi to the docks. I feel flushed. I know my cheeks are red and my eyes are shining. My hair is probably a mess from the headset and my hand is more than a little sweaty.

I don't care, though.

Riding in this sea plane next to Theo is the biggest thrill I've had in a long time. It makes me wonder if maybe I don't need to run away to explore the world. Maybe there's lots of adventure to be had right here in Argyle.

Maybe I could see the world with Theo by my side.

I shake my head to dispel the thought. This is *fake*. We're pretending. I'm doing it as a favor to Theo, and he's doing his best to protect me from the pressure of a potential engagement. He's buying himself time and helping me have a smooth exit from Argyle when this is all over.

That doesn't mean I can't enjoy these three weeks, though, does it?

As the workers on the dock help the pilot with ropes and staircases to secure the plane to the dock, I let out a breath.

"Wow," I sigh, pulling my headset off and smiling at Theo.

"Yeah." His eyes are shining, and a soft smile tugs at his lips.

We disembark the plane and walk down the dock as our suitcases are unloaded. An army of staff is waiting to help us off the plane, down the docks, and into the royal vehicle. I'm handed a warm towel to wipe my hands and face, and offered fresh fruit and champagne as we arrive next to a limousine.

I arch my eyebrows, glancing at Theo. "Is this what your life is like?"

He grins, shrugging. "More or less."

"You've been hiding this side of royal life from me."

"I've been showing you the real me instead."

A lump forms in my throat. I turn my attention to the champagne to hide the effect his words have on me. A flush creeps over my cheeks and my body thrums as I stand beside the Prince.

We're driven down a winding road to one of the royal villas. Even though I spent lots of time with the Princes of Argyle growing up, I didn't even know this property existed.

There's probably a lot of things I don't know about them.

As we pass through tall, ornate gates, I stare up at the tall palm trees that line the drive. Lush greenery surrounds us on all sides, with the clear blue sky arching high above us. A smile stretches over my lips and I lean against Theo's good shoulder.

"This is so beautiful," I sigh. "Thank you for having me. Feels like a holiday."

Theo doesn't answer. He only moves his arm to slide it over my shoulders, holding me close to his chest. We watch the trees part as a one-story villa appears in the distance. When the driver stops outside, the front door opens and a woman in a maid's uniform appears to help us into the villa.

As soon as I step inside, my jaw drops.

Marble, glass, and stainless steel everywhere. Every surface is gleaming. As I walk across the small, lush home, I spot floor-to-ceiling windows on the other side. My toes sink into a plush rug, and I run my fingers over a handmade basket full of shells. I smile. Outside, an infinity pool flows into the ocean beyond. The maid appears by my side, handing me another tall glass of champagne.

I could get used to this.

I accept the drink with a nod, my eyes widening as I turn to Theo.

"I thought you were here on official business."

He throws open the sliding glass door with one arm, wincing at the effort. His good hand goes to his shoulder, and I move to help him with the other door.

"This *is* official business. We'll be here on Arlian Island for three days, and then we're off to Zander for the fishing festival. It's my pre-coronation tour of the Kingdom, but it doesn't mean we can't enjoy ourselves."

I smile. Of the hundreds of islands that compose Argyle, I've only been to two or three. Arlian and Zander are two of the bigger ones, but I've never seen either of them.

Theo steps outside and a soft breeze flutters through the open door. As I walk out onto the pool deck, I peek at the white, sandy beach below. A hot tub steams over to the left, and the pool gurgles at my feet.

I shake my head. "I knew you were a prince, but I didn't realize this is what your life was like."

"You're not exactly from the other side of the tracks," Theo shoots back, grinning. "If I remember correctly, your father might be more popular than mine."

I shrug, laughing. "That doesn't mean we have the resources of the Crown behind us. This is next level. My father mostly gives our money away to fund his swimming school."

"Hence the need for you to make your own way." Theo sits down on one of the cushioned pool chairs, wincing at the pain in his shoulder again. I come to sit next to him on the same lounge chair, touching his sling with the tips of my fingers.

"Sore?"

He grunts in response. "This sling keeps rubbing against my skin."

I move his shirt collar to reveal red, raw skin at the base of his neck. I wince. "Theo, this looks painful."

"It is."

"Hold on."

I walk back inside, finding the maid to ask her for a first aid kit. She retrieves one from the cupboard and hands it to me.

"Need my help?" she asks, motioning to follow me.

I shake my head. "It's fine."

I'm used to doing things on my own. We have staff at my house, but nothing like this. Not waiting on us hand and foot. When I was younger we had more people around, but as we grew up and my father's work started to slow down, our household shrank.

Royalty is different. The staff that waits on Theo shows

real deference to him—and by extension, to me. It's strange, but not unpleasant.

The maid follows me outside. Theo is leaning against the back of the chair. He's taken his sling off and is cradling his arm against his stomach. I lift the first aid kit up and smile.

"Let me help you," I say.

The Prince nods, and then shifts his gaze to the maid. "We'll be fine, Desiree. Take the rest of the day off."

"But, Your Highness—"

"Take the day, Desiree. I can see that you've prepped the villa perfectly. Come back in the morning."

She curtsies, and right as she turns around, I see a smile split over her face. I guess even if you're working for royalty, it's still a job. Everyone appreciates a day off. I glance at the Prince, appreciating that he knows the names of almost all his staff. He treats them like real people, even though he's the future King.

I make my way over to Theo and take a seat next to him on the pool lounge chair again. Gently, I push his shirt off his shoulder. The area where his sling rubbed against his neck is raw and painful-looking. I get some ointment from the kit and gently dab it on. Theo jumps at the coolness of the salve and then sinks further into the chair.

"That feels so good," he groans.

The Prince closes his eyes as I dab the ointment on, my eyes wandering over his chest and shoulder. I undo another button in his shirt to reveal more of his skin, drifting my hand over the injured area.

I know I did it to save Theo from going overboard, but I hate that I'm the one to have caused him pain. I'm the one who dislocated his shoulder. I can't stand the thought of hurting him.

When my fingers slide over his skin, the Prince groans.

"Your touch feels so good," he says in a low growl. When his eyes open again, his gaze sends an arrow of heat through the pit of my stomach.

We said we'd pretend. We said that this wouldn't be real, and that we'd just be helping each other out. Him, to buy some time with his father and the coronation. Me, to make it easier to leave and protect me from unnecessary pressure.

We said that our kiss shouldn't happen again. It was a mistake.

But was it?

What if that kiss was the one real thing about this? What if being with Theo is as right as it feels?

The Prince's gaze is intoxicating. Touching his bare skin sends a shiver straight to my gut, igniting fire in my veins. Embers swirl in his eyes as he stares at me, his tongue sliding out to lick his lips.

We're balancing on the edge of a precipice. I know we are.

Either we fall head-first into disaster, or this is the start of something beautiful. Pretending to get engaged to him could be the best or worst thing I've ever done.

Which will it be?

Right now, the only thing on my mind is how much I want him. We're alone here, in this villa tucked away on the edge of the world. The luxury and solitude around us heighten the feeling that everything about this is right.

Who cares about the rest of the world? Who cares about our past, and our future? Who cares about our families and our obligations?

The only thing that matters is Prince Theo and me, the fact that his lips look irresistibly kissable, and that his body was carved from something divine.

I can't resist my desires anymore.

Leaning forward, I kiss the Prince. As soon as our lips

touch, fire roars to life in my core. I'm sick of fighting this feeling in my heart, when this feeling is the only thing that's ever been good.

I'm tired of torturing myself about Luca, when he's only brought pain into my life. I'm sick of pretending that I don't want Theo. That I still want to leave as desperately as I did a week ago. That he doesn't make me feel more alive than anyone else ever has.

So, I let go.

I give in.

I surrender to my feelings and let the desire take over. I kiss the Crown Prince of Argyle with all the force of my feelings, showing him what I really feel for him. Tangling my fingers into his hair, I crush my lips against his and moan into his mouth.

Swinging my leg over to straddle Theo, I try my best to avoid his bad shoulder while simultaneously pressing my body against his.

His good hand grips me tight, his fingers sinking into the flesh at my hip.

"Cara," he groans. "Are you sure?"

I pull away slightly, staring deep into his ocean-blue eyes. "Surer than I've ever been about anything, ever."

11

____

THEO

I wish I hadn't dislocated my shoulder. The things I want to do to Cara require the use of both my arms. The pleasure I want to give her needs my full health and attention.

As it is, I can barely move. I wrap my uninjured arm around her and pull her close, wincing as she nudges against my bad shoulder.

"Sorry," she says, drawing away from me. I hate the distance. She frowns. "I can stop, if you want."

"The last thing I want you to do is stop."

Cara rolls her hips against me. I groan. I can feel the fire radiating from her core, her dress riding up to her hips. My fingers trail along her thighs, feeling the slight peach fuzz on her skin. I let my fingers drift over the waistband of her panties, moving to touch the heat between her legs.

Yesterday, we said we'd pretend. I knew we were lying to ourselves.

Today, this feels very, very real.

Whatever is happening between Cara and me is unstoppable. We're a runaway train, roaring down the tracks toward certain destruction.

Nothing good can come of this.

But do I care? Not in the slightest.

My good hand reaches down between her legs, and I groan when I feel the wetness soaking her panties. Cara lets out a soft sigh, kissing my lips as she furiously unbuttons my shirt. She pushes it open, being gentle around my injured shoulder. Rocking her panties against my hand, she groans as her hands splay over my chest.

I don't even care that my shoulder hurts. What is pain? The only thing that matters is my rock-hard cock doing its best to break free from my pants.

That, and the wetness soaking through Cara's underwear.

Pushing the ruined strip of fabric to the side, I drag my fingers through her honey. She moans again, and I swear it's the sweetest sound I've ever heard. I can't keep my eyes off her. She rocks herself against my hand as her lips drop open. Her nails dig into my chest and another wave of agony passes through my shoulder.

I still don't care about it.

When I slip a finger inside her, keeping my palm pressed against her clit, Cara lets out the sexiest noise I've ever heard. She looks down at me, eyes dark and full of sin.

The pool lounge chair creaks beneath us, but I can't bring myself to care. If it breaks, it breaks. It'll break while I'm experiencing the closest thing to heaven on earth.

"Theo..." Cara whispers, rolling her hips against me. I can feel the clenching of her walls and the wetness dripping out of her. She's the sexiest woman I've ever seen, and right now, she's all mine.

It doesn't matter that we might regret this. It doesn't matter that we're supposed to be pretending. It doesn't matter that this could be a big mistake.

It's happening, and it's the best thing I could have asked

for. Ever since she stepped onto the sailboat with me, my mind has been plagued with thoughts of Cara. Of what I want to do to her. What I wish she'd do to me.

Now, it's happening.

Cara rides my hand, reaching down to touch her clit as I slip another finger inside her. I watch her play with herself, my cock throbbing at the thought of what she's doing.

"Come for me, Cara," I growl, mesmerized by the movement of her hand as it dances over her own clit. My voice is a low growl as it scrapes out of my throat. "Come all over my hand and then come again on my cock."

A smile tugs at Cara's lips as a gasp slips through them. She likes when I say dirty things to her, and that turns me on even more. She moves her hand away from her bud for just a moment. Her eyes beg me for more, even though she's the one teasing herself. I wish I had two hands. I wish I could give her everything.

Cara leans over and kisses me fiercely. Her hand moves to her clit again, and I can tell by the trembling in her body that she's close.

I'm so hard I think I might explode. She's grinding on top of me, bringing herself to orgasm. Her wetness is dripping down my hand as she pleasures herself, the nails of her other hand digging into my chest. If I thought I'd experienced pleasure before, I was wrong.

Nothing comes close to this, and she hasn't even touched me yet.

Then, Cara stops. With dark eyes and even darker intentions, she lifts herself off me and moves to unbutton my pants.

My voice catches as a lump forms in my throat. All I can do is watch.

When she releases me from my clothing, my cock springs

up toward her. Cara grins, catching it in her soft hand. Then, she strokes me, and I know I'm not going to last long.

A growl rumbles through my chest as I watch this gorgeous, intoxicating woman stroke my cock. It's leaking already. She rubs her thumb over my tip, spreading my precum over my crown. I moan, leaning my head back as heat blooms inside me. The pressure in the pit of my stomach mounts.

She feels too good. My hand is still covered in her honey, and she's getting messy with my cock. I fucking love that she isn't afraid. Not afraid to touch me. To touch herself. To let me know exactly what she wants.

She doesn't care that it's messy. She wants it that way.

As always, Cara is her own person. She doesn't treat me like her future King. She doesn't hesitate and dither about what she thinks I want. She just shows me exactly what she needs.

Then, Cara does something I don't expect.

Kneeling above me, she tugs her panties to the side and positions herself over me.

"Cara—" I manage to say, choking on my own words. The tip of my cock brushes against her slit, and another wave of lust crashes into me.

We shouldn't be doing this. In no universe should I be having sex with Cara Shoal right now.

But my cock is hard and throbbing, and she's sopping wet, perched on top of it. Her hand still strokes my shaft as she rubs my crown up and down her slit. Cara's eyes are demanding, her full bottom lip sucked between her teeth.

I can't take it anymore. It's too much teasing. Too much waiting. Too much wanting. Too much holding back.

"Cara," I growl.

"Yes, Your Highness?" Her eyes flash as a wicked smile tugs at her lips.

"Sit on my fucking cock." The command is ripped from my throat before I can stop myself. I couldn't hold back if I tried.

I want Cara. She wants me.

We're not fighting it any longer.

12

CARA

THE PRINCE'S order sends a jolt of desire piercing through my body. My nipples pebble at the command, and I'm almost embarrassed at how much I love the sound of his dirty words.

Then, I do as he wishes.

I sink down on top of my future King, sheathing him inside me. As soon as I feel him enter me, I let out a gasp. Rocking my hips to feel him deeper, I have to throw my head back. Then, I still. My body takes a moment to accommodate to his girth, and a soft smile stretches over my lips.

This is what I've been wanting since that night on the sailboat. Prince Theo's cock buried deep inside me. His hands on my body. The total ecstasy that accompanies every touch.

It feels more right than I could have imagined. We were made for each other. This is exactly where he's supposed to be.

Inside me.

As I start gently rocking my hips, the Prince lets out a low moan. The sound makes heat bloom in the pit of my stomach. I clench my thighs, grinding harder into him. He lets out another moan, sending a wave of heat flooding through my veins. It starts in the pit of my stomach and spreads outward, ripping through my body like a wildfire.

The Prince groans. Every sound he makes sends another wave of lust crashing into me. The look in his eyes tells me he wants more. He's been waiting for this, too.

He's enjoying this as much as I am.

Leaning my hands on his chest, I close my eyes for just a moment. Feeling him inside me is so deliciously wrong I can't stop myself from almost giving in to the urge to let go. I want to come. I want to feel the release of an orgasm that feels like it's been building for years.

I want to give it to *him*.

Theo reaches up to slip the strap of my dress off my shoulder. His hand drifts over to my breast, teasing it with his thumb. He's barely touching me, but the slightest drift of his fingers sends electricity jumping through my veins.

As my hips rock back and forth, I slip off the other strap of my dress. Theo sighs, cupping my breast.

I do the same to my other breast, loving the way his eyes darken when I do it. I can tell he likes watching me touch myself. I tweak my nipple between my thumb and forefinger. His lips drop open and his cock throbs.

"Pleasure yourself," he commands, flicking his eyes between my legs.

Am I *supposed* to love it when he orders me around like that? Is it wrong that the sound of his voice makes me want to melt? Burn? Obey?

I've always been independent. I've always wanted to explore the world and see what else was out there. I've collected treasures from everywhere and anywhere. Scraps of this and that, precious to only me.

I've always thought of myself as someone who wanted to explore.

Right now, though? The only thing I want to explore is Theo's body. The only world that holds any interest to me is the universe inside his eyes. The only treasures I want to collect are his moans. His kisses. His touch.

Reaching down between my legs, I start teasing my clit. Theo lets out a low exhale as the pool lounge chair creaks beneath us again. I brace myself against it, riding Theo as I pleasure myself.

The Prince's bad arm is pinned against his chest while his other hand drifts over my body, teasing everywhere he touches. When he lets his fingers slide down my side and over my thigh, a trail of goosebumps follows. I know I'm near the edge.

Alone with him, at the edge of the world, Theo gives me everything.

He drives himself deeper inside me as I ride him, and my pleasure crests. My orgasm isn't timid. It doesn't hesitate. It slams into me with all the force of my waiting and wanting. It makes me keel over, sinking my fingers into the Prince's uninjured arm to keep from falling off.

Heat rips through my body. It blazes through my veins like molten metal, electrifying every inch of my trembling body. A gasp slips through my lips as the Prince grunts, his fingers gripping my thigh so hard it feels like the only thing keeping me upright.

It's an orgasm like never before. It's a release from everything I've been holding inside me, and a promise that I'll always look for more.

More lust.

More mind-melting, body-burning pleasure.

More Theo.

I'm so busy riding my own wave of lust that I barely notice the Prince stiffening underneath me. His whole body tenses.

Vaguely, at the back of my mind, I realize he's coming, too. I feel his shaft growing harder and his fingers grip me tighter. His grunts become more labored.

"I'm going to come," he groans, his hand digging into me.

Does he want me to get off? Does he think that's even possible for me to do right now? No part of my body is cooperating with my brain. I couldn't move if I tried.

So, I don't try.

I rock my hips again, riding the last wave of my pleasure as my body burns up.

The Prince empties himself inside me, and I can't help but smile. Another, smaller wave of pleasure washes over me, bathing me in a soft glow of bliss as I try to catch my breath.

I like the feeling of his orgasm. I like knowing that it happened with me. Because of me. Inside me.

As my vision clears, I see the Prince's chest heaving. He releases my thigh and rubs his injured shoulder, groaning.

"You hurt?" I ask between breaths.

He shakes his head. "I'm fine."

"You don't look fine."

"It was worth it." A smile tugs at his lips. Soft warmth spreads through my chest, and I finally climb off the Prince's lap.

Stumbling, I catch myself against another pool chair as a laugh slips through my lips. My legs feel like jelly and my brain hasn't quite managed to function normally again, either. Pink, fluffy clouds of brain fog obscure my every thought, and all I can do is collapse against the other chair as I struggle to catch my breath.

The Prince chuckles, glancing over at me. "You'll end up like me. Just two injured idiots touring around the Kingdom, pretending we know what we're doing."

"Who are you calling an idiot?" I grin at him, leaning my head against the back of the chair.

Vaguely, at the back of my mind, I realize that I just had unprotected sex with the Crown Prince of Argyle. Pink, fluffy brain fog chases the thought away.

It'll be fine. I just had my period recently, didn't I?

It's just one time.

But as soon as the thought crosses my mind, I know that I don't want it to be only one time at all. The Prince and I stare at each other from our respective chairs as the waves crash on the shores below. As the clouds in my head clear, I hear seagulls squawking and the pool filter gurgling next to me. Wind rustles through the trees, and a soft, warm breeze wraps the Prince's scent all around me.

No, I don't want this to be the only time we make love. A flush blooms over my cheeks as all my familiar fears and insecurities swell up inside me. I blink rapidly, looking away from Theo's face.

This shouldn't happen more than once, but I still hope it will. I can't marry him, even though my family wants me to. We can't be together. There are too many things standing between us. Too many obstacles to our happiness. Too much baggage to drag around.

Theo senses the shift in me and lifts himself off the chair.

"Come on," he commands in his familiar voice as the future King of Argyle. "Let's shower."

He nods to an outdoor shower on the opposite side of the pool, and I push my fears away. For now, I'm here. I'm with Theo. I can ignore the future looming grin in the distance, when we tell our family that we won't go through with the marriage.

For now, we're pretending, and that's enough for me.

13

___

THEO

WATCHING Cara slip her thin sundress off makes my breath catch. In the solitude of our royal villa on the Island of Arlian, our relationship feels almost real. We're tucked away on the edge of the Atlantic, with no one but seagulls to keep us company.

When we're together, I'm whole. I've spent so long thinking I could become King on my own that I haven't stopped to wonder if I might be missing something.

Love. Laughter. The companionship of a good woman.

Ever since my mother left, my father has shrunk away from his responsibilities. Our relationships with the neighboring countries deteriorated, and trade agreements have expired and turned sour.

As Cara turns on the faucet and tests the temperature of the water, I start to wonder if maybe this relationship is exactly what I need.

Argyle isn't a behemoth of a Kingdom that needs its old, dying King. It's a bright, vibrant nation that needs new life. New trade. New industry.

A new King.

Maybe a new Queen, too.

Have I been so focused on fulfilling my duties and being responsible that I've neglected the importance of being happy?

Cara glances at me, nodding to the shower. "It's warm now. Is your sling okay to go in the water?"

I nod. "It's fine."

My eyes drift down Cara's body. She's curvy, lithe, and completely breathtaking. She's athletic and feminine all at once, probably thanks to being born a swimmer. With my uninjured arm, I push her long, brown mane of hair to one side and drop a kiss on the back of her neck.

She sighs, leaning her head back against me. I lay a trail of kisses down her shoulder, reaching around her body to feel her skin beneath my hand. Cupping her breast, I kiss her neck again, then her ear, her jaw, and when she turns her head, her lips.

Every movement feels natural. Underneath the stream of water in the shower, I kiss this woman like she's going to be my wife.

I know it's all fake, but right now it feels real. Our worries fade into the distance, and I just hold her close and kiss her with the strength of my passion.

We wash each other, staring down at the strip of beach that belongs to the royal family—to me.

It could belong to Cara, too, if she wanted it. As her hands drift over my chest, she spreads suds and soap over my body. She washes my injured shoulder with the gentlest touch, flicking her eyes to mine a few times to make sure she's not hurting me.

She *cares*.

Cares about hurting me. Cares about hurting my brother by being here.

All the while, she pushes her own dreams aside.

Should I really be asking her to do that? Here I am, having my body washed by the most beautiful girl in Argyle, dreaming of making her my wife.

But she told me herself she doesn't want that. She doesn't want to be my wife. She doesn't want to stay in Argyle. She wants to explore, to sing, to travel.

The only way I can give her that is if I let her go.

The royal life is regimented and planned. I'll travel, sure, but it won't be the way she wants to travel. She won't be sticking her arms out of a convertible and sailing the high seas.

If this relationship were to become real, I'd be condemning Cara to a life of pomp and circumstance, devoid of the spontaneity she craves. It would be the life I've been living since I was a child—duty, responsibility, and the weight of the crown.

"What's going on in that big, princely head of yours?" Cara chucks my chin as she arches an eyebrow. "You look like you're carrying the world on your shoulders."

"I was just thinking about how beautiful you are," I answer, dropping my lips to hers.

The shower soaks us both as we kiss, and the sun dips below the horizon. Pulling away from me, Cara stares at the sunset as a sigh slips through her lips. She leans her head against my good shoulder, and we stand there in silence.

Comfortable silence. Companionable silence.

A silence that I could get used to, if Cara wanted it.

Then, she pulls away and turns off the shower. "I'll get wrinkly at this rate," she grins. "Come on. I'm hungry."

When we make our way inside, wrapped in white, fluffy towels, the air conditioning is blasting through the villa. Cara shivers, finding the remote to turn it off.

"No need for that," she huffs, shivering.

I love that Cara is comfortable around me. She treats me like any normal person. She isn't scared to turn off the air conditioner without asking me. She doesn't defer to my preference for everything.

She's her own, whole person, not some shell of a human created to do my bidding.

Right now, she has her head stuck in the refrigerator. I stare at her ass as she pulls out some of the pre-made food the royal chef prepared before our arrival.

"I could *definitely* get used to this," Cara says, flipping open a container to reveal delicious spiced chicken and rice. "This is better than my cooking for sure."

I grin, grabbing the fork she hands me and dig in. I ignore the tremor in my heart at the thought of Cara getting used to this life.

That would mean she wanted this life. That she chose it.

That she chose *me*.

THE NEXT DAY has a full schedule of royal activities. Cara accompanies me as a guest, staying out of the spotlight. As we visit the local elementary school and then the hospital, I find myself glancing at her and wishing she were beside me for all these photo opportunities instead of staying in the background.

We haven't gone public with the engagement, for obvious reasons—it's not real. An engagement to Cara Shoal would cause a splash, and a breakup would cause an even bigger one. We can't let anyone know about our supposed engagement.

She's only here to buy me some time with Dante.

But I still steal a glance or two her way. When we visit the children's ward in the hospital, I watch as Cara reads a story to two of the kids, who laugh and lean against her. Cara's cheeks flush as she reads the book aloud, making different voices for the characters and slowly gathering more and more kids around her. They flock to her, and my heart thumps.

She's good, she's kind—and everyone can see it. What if a couple of those kids were ours? I push the thought aside.

When the day is over, we head back to the villa. Cara leans her head against the back of the car seat, sighing.

"That was exhausting, but nice."

"Yeah?"

She nods. "I know no one was there to see me, but I still felt lucky. All those kids at the hospital have gone through so much, but they're still smiling and laughing."

"Because of you," I grin.

"What? No." She shakes her head. "They were so brave."

"They loved you."

"They were excited to meet their future King."

"And Queen." The word slips out. I clear my throat to cover it up, looking away from Cara.

She's not the future Queen. No one knows about our supposed upcoming engagement, and no one was looking at her as my bride.

But she was there, and she was loved.

I never saw my mother act like Cara did, or be received as openly as Cara was. I never saw kids flock to her, and photographers snap pictures of her.

My mother was cold. She cheated on my father and then she left. I haven't spoken to her in years. I guess, in a way, I always assumed that becoming King would be easier if I did it on my own. I'd protect myself from going through the heartbreak that my father went through.

Cara's different, though. She would make a great queen.

But *it's. Not. Real.* How many times do I have to remind myself of that?

I stare at the island passing us by as our driver winds through the lush countryside. We drive over rolling hills, and the true sense of responsibility starts to weight on me. This is my kingdom.

Then, Cara's hand slips into mine. I turn to meet her gaze, and a soft smile stares back at me. Her eyes speak volumes, even though we don't say a word.

She's here beside me, and that's real enough for now.

The car comes to a stop and the driver opens my door.

"Your Highness," he nods, helping me out of the vehicle. "Do you need anything else? I've had the staff prepare dinner for you. The chef and maid are still here for your dinner service, but I've told them you won't be needing them afterward."

"Thank you. We'll be fine."

Cara appears at my side, not having waited for the driver to open her door. She smiles at him before slipping her arm around my waist to help me into the villa.

14

CARA

THE LINES on Theo's face betray how much his shoulder hurts him. As he sinks down onto the plush sofa in the villa's living room, I watch him dig around his pocket for his bottle of painkillers.

I hate seeing him like this, and it surprises me just how much I care.

Sitting down next to him, I lay my hand on his thigh as we watch the chef and the rest of the staff prepare our dinner. Theo lets out a long breath. He closes his eyes, and within moments, he's asleep.

My heart squeezes.

Of course I care about him—we've been friends our whole lives. Even when I was with Luca, Theo meant a lot to me.

But it's like he said, something shifted between us on that sailboat. Things changed when we kissed, whether I want to admit it or not. Today, seeing him acting like the King of Argyle, I saw another side of him.

He's not just the strait-laced Prince who does his duty. It runs deeper than just doing what he's supposed to do. It's his passion. His calling. He's dedicated and caring, and he'll be a great king.

Maybe, just maybe, there's room in that story for me.

But is that what I want, or am I just being blinded by the luxury of the royal life?

As we wait for our dinner to be prepared, I drift off to a place between wakefulness and sleep. My mind runs away with all the possibilities that could be. If we didn't have the weight of the past between us. If I hadn't been promised to his brother. If he wasn't going to be King.

A future with Theo would be bright. I liked seeing him interact with his subjects today. He had a glow in his eye, and he made sure to give every single person his full attention. It made us incredibly late for every stop on the schedule—and exhausted him in the process—but it showed me the kind of King he's going to be.

He's not a slave to his responsibilities—he embraces them. I used to think Theo was a bit boring, and I assumed it was because he knew he would be King. I never realized that 'boring' for me was fulfilling for him.

Once we tell our parents that we're not going through with the engagement, all this will be left behind. I'm sure my mother will make sure that I leave Argyle, then. I'll have ruined my chances with not only one, but two royal princes of Argyle.

That's not what bothers me, though. Pain pierces my chest when I think of someone else being beside him after I leave. Will another woman take my place after this fake engagement is over?

Theo rustles beside me, blinking his eyes open. "What time is it?"

"You've been asleep for about three minutes."

He chuckles, rubbing his face with his hand. "Felt like hours."

"I think the food's almost ready."

I help the Prince to his feet, and then enjoy a quiet meal with him. I've noticed that since we've been at this villa, we've shared more silence than we did before. Even on the sailboat, when we were quiet, there was underlying tension.

Now, it's just peaceful.

When dinner is over, I can tell that Theo's tired. He dismisses the staff and then trudges up to the ensuite bathroom. We brush our teeth, and then I hover at the doorway, unsure whether or not he wants me to come into the bedroom with him.

Last night, we slept in the same bed, but then again, we'd just had sex. Today, there hasn't been any of that.

Maybe Theo wants his privacy?

But after he pulls off his socks, he glances at me. "What are you doing standing in the doorway? Get over here."

"I didn't know if you'd want to sleep alone tonight. You look tired."

"Being with you is better than being alone." His eyes shine when he says the words. Simple words, but with rich meaning.

My heart thumps. It's like it's knocking against my bones, asking me to listen. Listen to the pulse thudding in my veins. Listen to the fickle, fragile organ in my chest as it tells me to let myself fall for Theo.

With a lump in my throat and my pulse quickening, I strip down to my underwear and slip under the covers. Theo groans as his head hits the pillow, and then extends his uninjured arm toward me.

"Get in here," he groans, his eyelids already heavy. "This is your house."

I snuggle into the Prince's chest, letting out a sigh. My house. My home. The one place where I feel safe and welcome.

Theo's arms.

THE NEXT MORNING, Theo is already awake when I get up. I find him in the kitchen, hanging up the phone. He flashes a smile before handing a steaming mug to me.

"Change of plans today."

"Oh?" I sip the hot coffee. He put lots of cream and sugar in it, just the way I like it.

"We're going to Wreck Island."

"I thought we were supposed to stay here for three days and then go to Zander?"

"That's why it's called a change of plans."

"Ha-ha," I say sarcastically, rolling my eyes. I can't hide my smile, though, and Theo lays a kiss on my temple. I turn to wrap my arms around his waist, angling my face up to his. "Didn't know you were the spontaneous type."

"Maybe you shouldn't underestimate me."

When his lips touch mine, a tendril of heat flames to life in my core. He never fails to make me feel alive. Womanly. Desired.

Seeing the look in my eye, Theo grins. He intertwines his fingers with mine and leads me to the sofa.

"Sit."

Once again, I'm powerless to his commands. I sit down, my eyes glued to Theo's face. A wicked flash crosses his eyes as his brows arch.

"Time for breakfast," he grins. With one hand, he tugs at my panties. I help him get them off, then watch the Prince toss the scrap of fabric over his shoulder.

Giggling, I shimmy my hips down to the edge of the sofa and reach for the waistband of his boxers. Pushing my hand away, though, Theo shakes his head.

"Not this morning."

"Why?" I whine, reaching for him.

"Because I'm your future King, and I said so." He kneels on the floor in front of me, pushing my legs wide. For once, I don't mind him pulling the King card. Propping his uninjured arm against my thigh, the Prince drops his head between my legs.

I gasp, closing my eyes. Heat explodes through my core, spreading heat throughout my body. I squeeze my legs against him and then stop when I feel him wince.

"Shoulder," he says, his lips glistening with my wetness.

"Sorry," I whisper.

Without answer, the Prince drops his lips to me again.

Sparks flame to life inside me. Desire and lust swirl in my center, coaxed out by the Prince's touch. By his tongue. By his lips. By the fact that he seems to be enjoying this almost as much as I am.

I tangle my fingers into his thick hair, tugging him into me. He grunts, lapping up my honey and shifting his hand to touch me. When he slips his fingers inside me, I moan.

Whatever is going on between the Prince and me, I'm powerless to resist. I can tell myself that I shouldn't do this. That it's wrong. That I'm leaving as soon as it's over.

But I'm lying to myself.

How can I leave? How can I turn my back on Theo? How can I deny myself the one thing that has brought me joy in over three years? I feel like myself for the first time since as long as I can remember.

Even before, when I was with Luca, it wasn't like this.

Electric. Frantic. It didn't make my whole body feel like it was melting.

With Luca, it was just...expected. That's what was supposed to happen.

With Theo, it's more than that. It feels wrong, but oh so right. It feels like we should be holding back, but that only makes me want to give him more. Everything. *Anything*.

When I come, my back arches and my hands grip his hair. He doesn't stop until I go limp, finally lifting his gaze to meet mine. A smile stretches over his lips as he lays a soft kiss just below my belly button.

"There. Good morning, beautiful."

I mumble something unintelligible.

The Prince chuckles, reaching his hand down to his crotch. His bulge is unmistakable, but instead of letting me reach for it, he nods to the kitchen. "Let's eat."

FOR THE NEXT couple of hours, Theo is painfully out of reach. As soon as we finish our breakfast, the staff arrives at the villa to clean up after us. We get dressed and head to the waiting car, and are whisked back to the sea plane pier.

On the drive there, my fingers go on an exploratory mission over Theo's body. He grunts in warning, catching my hand and bringing it to his lips.

"Not here."

"Where?" I ask, frustrated. The privacy screen is up between us and the driver. We have at least ten minutes before we get to the pier. Ten minutes is long enough. I want to make him feel as good as he made me feel this morning. Maybe, selfishly, I want him to touch me again. His hands make me feel alive. His touch is life-giving. His kiss is magic.

He doesn't answer. He just tangles his fingers in mine and smiles, waiting for the car to bring us to the plane.

Even when we're in the air and I'm marveling at the water below us, I can still feel a whisper of heat coursing through my veins. Glancing over my shoulder, I catch Theo's gaze. It's full of heat and wanting, and it only makes my desire for him grow.

Still, though, he keeps his hands to himself.

This morning was just a tease.

When we land, Theo has a gleam in his eye. "This way," he says.

"Where are we? What are we doing? How long will we be here? Should I have brought my bag?"

"Relax, Cara."

He threads his fingers through mine and leads me down the pier toward the shore. From there, he waves away the car that waits for us and nods toward the town. "We'll walk," he says.

A bodyguard trails behind us, but Theo doesn't seem too bothered about being exposed.

Narrow, colorful streets greet us. People stop us every few feet to take pictures and shake Theo's hand. He keeps me close, introducing me to everyone that we meet.

It feels like we're together. I suppose in a way, we are. But it feels like we're *really* together. Like we'll be together even after this trip is over.

"This way," Theo says when there's a break in the selfies and baby-kissing that seems to happen anytime he's in public.

He leads me down a narrow alleyway with the bodyguard behind us. From there, we twist and turn through the streets and finally end up at a nondescript door. There's no sign to tell me where we are, and no discerning features on the door or building. It's just a brown door on a colorful concrete building next to lots of other brown doors on colorful concrete buildings.

Theo smiles at me. "You ready?"

"I guess. It would help if I knew what I was getting ready for."

The Prince just laughs, pushes the door open, and we step through.

BEING part of the royal family means lots of charitable work. Most of my life has been spent giving—time, money, attention.

It never felt real, though. Even though we say we're giving, and we have countless photo opportunities and events that promote our family, it always feels like a way to gain popularity. Charitable work, for the royal family of Argyle, isn't an actual genuine way to give back. It's an exchange. We give to charity, and we take the boost in public opinion.

Walking into this music studio is genuine. Changing my plans so Cara can meet one of Argyle's best musicians is real. That's giving. Something that I'm doing only to make her happy, and nothing else.

The look on Cara's face when she sees the gold records on the wall is priceless. Her eyes widen and her full, lush lips drop open. As we walk down a short hallway toward the room beyond, Cara grabs my arm.

"Is this what I think it is?"

"That depends what you think it is," I laugh.

She digs her fingernails into my arm until I grunt in pain.

"Sorry," Cara says as if she hadn't realized what she was doing. She drops her hand and steps forward to look around the room. "Is this Prudence Halloway's studio? I heard about this place. Apparently, John Lennon was here with Yoko Ono in the seventies."

I point to the wall, where photos of other famous singers and musicians stare back at us. "A bunch of others, too."

Cara sucks in a breath, shaking her head.

We're in a music studio. It's small, but you can sense the layers of music and memories that coat the place. Guitars and basses hang on the walls, and a glass-walled booth is tucked in the corner.

From behind a beaded curtain, a woman emerges.

Not just any woman. Argyle's most famous and most celebrated musician. Prudence Halloway was the voice of my father's generation. Now, her hair is a mix of grey, white, and black, twisted into long locks that perch on top of her head. Few wrinkles are etched into her smooth skin—just a few smile lines and shallow crows' feet near her eyes. She's laughed a lot in her life.

Dark brown eyes crinkle as she smiles at us, spreading her arms toward Cara.

"You must be Miss Shoal. I cheered for your father at the Olympics."

"You know my father?"

Prudence laughs, shaking her head. "No. But I cheered for him."

"I feel like I should curtsy." Cara glances at me.

Prudence smiles again, and she wraps her arms around Cara in a warm hug. "Come in. Let me hear you sing."

"Wait, what?"

"Isn't that why you're here? His Highness told me you wanted to make music with me. Not the phone call I was expecting yesterday." Prudence's whole aura is warm, and her presence is calming. Cara's shoulders relax, and I sink into an old sofa near the wall.

"I can't sing," Cara says, shaking her head.

"I don't believe you." Prudence arches an eyebrow.

Cara smiles, a blush creeping over her cheeks.

Prudence grabs a guitar from the wall and props it on her lap, arching an eyebrow at Cara. "Let go of it all, Cara. Sing with me."

The old woman strums the guitar with a smile on her face, and I watch as Prudence coaxes Cara out of her shell. As soon as they start to play, I'm transported to my childhood. My father used to love this music. He'd play it in the palace at full volume, humming along to Prudence's melodies.

That was before my mother cheated on him. Before she left. Before he fell ill.

For the first time in my royal career, as I watch Cara smile wide and finally sing her first note, I feel like I've done something good.

I'm not here to have a photo with someone. I'm not here to kiss babies and make the citizens of Argyle think I'm a worthy Prince. I'm just here for Cara. To show her that I care about her voice, her singing. To show her that music is still alive in this kingdom, even if it doesn't exist in her house.

To prove to her that she doesn't need a fancy education at an expensive school to sing. She doesn't need permission from anyone to find her voice.

We stay there for almost two hours. I relax on the sofa, listening to the two women harmonize. As I listen to Cara sing, I realize how much I missed that sound. She used to hum and sing and shout all the time when we were kids.

Now, her voice is fuller. It's rounder. It's slightly deeper, but it's just as beautiful as I remember.

Most importantly, she's laughing. Smiling. Her *eyes* are shining. I can see in her face how much this means to her, and it makes me feel good to bring her here.

Not for me or my reputation. Not for the royal family.

Simply for Cara.

When we leave, Prudence gives Cara her personal phone number. The two women hug each other again, and we leave the old Argylian singer in her studio as we step out into the sunshine again.

"Oh, Theo," Cara says, hooking her elbow around mine and leaning her head against my shoulder. "That was incredible."

"You have a beautiful voice." My voice is tight, and it's hard to speak past the lump in my throat. I want to say so much more. I wish I could tell her how moved I was, listening to them, or how much joy it brought me to see her happy.

Instead, I say nothing. We just walk, arm in arm, back toward the pier.

"Thank you," Cara says, pausing to look at me.

I turn to face her. My heart stutters as I see the sun shining on her skin. She's glowing. Her long, brown hair frames her face so perfectly, she looks almost ethereal. An angel sent here to show me what really matters in life. Her eyes glimmer in the sunlight, and emotion threatens to knock me back.

In that moment, standing in a narrow street on one of Argyle's smaller islands, I know that Cara means more to me than I realized.

I want to see her look this happy all the time. It *matters* to me that she's happy. Not as a friend. Not as a citizen of Argyle. Not because it's my duty to care, as King. I care about her. Deeply. Unconditionally.

More than I realized.

"It was nothing," I finally manage to say. "I wanted to do something you'd enjoy on this tour. I know the official events are boring."

"Nothing is boring with you," she smiles. "But no one's ever done anything like that for me. Mother wouldn't even let me have voice lessons. She said it was beneath our family's station."

"Prudence seemed to think you did well."

"She was amazing, wasn't she?" Cara's face breaks into a smile as her eyes get a faraway look in them. "It was like every note she sang was just dripping with emotion. She could convey so much with her voice." Cara shakes her head. "I've never felt so excited about singing. Even though I've always loved it, I... I don't know. That was incredible."

"There are lots of good singers in Argyle," I smile, tucking a strand of hair behind Cara's ear. "You're one of them."

A blush reddens her cheeks and the emotion inside me swells.

This is what I want. That shine in Cara's eyes. The life and happiness bubbling up inside her. The inspiration in her voice.

I want to make Cara Shoal happy.

Even though we're out on the street and anyone could see us, I can't help myself. I lean forward and brush my lips against Cara's, kissing her in the middle of this colorful, narrow street. She melts into me, placing her hands on my chest as I deepen our kiss—and I feel whole.

It's not fake. It's not temporary.

What I feel for Cara is real, and it's not going away...

...I just hope she feels it, too.

16

CARA

Being on tour with Theo is like living in a dream. I'm waited on hand and foot as we fly from beautiful royal villa to beautiful royal villa. The people of Argyle are adoring and happy, and I get to experience a new side of the Kingdom that I haven't had a chance to see before.

I've lived a sheltered life. Even though my upbringing was comfortable, I realize that I haven't really seen much of my own home Kingdom.

I haven't seen the crowded markets and the hidden beaches. I haven't seen the rich history that unites every island.

Maybe that's why I've been wanting to run away—because as the days pass, I realize that's what I've been doing. Running away. Packing my bags and jumping ship, so I don't have to deal with the oppressive weight of my family's expectations.

I don't feel like running away anymore, because for the first time, my family's expectations are aligning with what I want—Theo.

We spend a week tangled in bedsheets together when

we're in private. During the day, we visit all corners of the Kingdom and connect with the people that Theo will one day rule.

One day soon. I see the weight of Theo's duties carried on his broad shoulders. Sometimes, when no one is looking, I see the lines deepen on his face. He cares about his people, and he wants to be a good king.

I didn't understand it before. When we were kids, I thought Theo was too responsible. Too boring. I didn't understand that through him runs a deep well of kindness and a sense of importance. Like every action he takes is significant.

Now, I get it. Theo has a purpose. He has the one thing that I've wanted to find—what I thought I would discover if I left Argyle. He knows what he needs to do in life, and every action he takes is carefully considered to align with his duties.

A week into our tour, we visit a small nursing home on one of the more populated islands of the Kingdom. An old man with a shock of white hair and mottled skin smiles at Theo, revealing big gaps in his teeth. He waves the Prince closer to his wheelchair, his smile widening.

"Tell your father I'm very proud of him, Your Highness," the old man says, patting Theo's hand.

"I will, sir."

One of the nurses apologizes and tries to quiet the old man down. The old man waves her away.

"He did great things in this Kingdom when he was a young man. It'll be your time, soon."

Theo nods politely.

The old man leans back in his wheelchair, staring at the Prince. "You have to be strong. Make sure you have a good woman by your side, because being a leader is a heavy burden to bear alone. Your father could have continued building this country up if he'd had a faithful wife by his side. It was only after she betrayed him that things went to shit."

"Thomas!" the nurse chides, her cheeks turning bright red. "That's no way to talk about our royal family. Your Highness, I—"

"It's fine," Theo says, smiling sadly. "He's right."

Theo's eyes slide to me, and a dagger pierces my heart. In that brief glance, I realize what I've been afraid to admit to myself: I want to be the good woman by his side. The one to support him, to help him bear the weight of the crown.

Not because it's the Crown, and I feel like it's my duty to help. But because it's Theo who has to bear it.

My priorities are shifting. Day by day, I realize I don't want to run away. I don't need to leave to find myself. There are things right here in Argyle that are worth staying for.

That evening, when Theo and I are alone in the royal villa, Theo has a faraway look on his face. We're sitting on a plush sofa, watching the waves crash on the shore. I thread my fingers through the Prince's.

"You're going to make a great king," I say softly.

Theo turns his head to glance at me, smiling. "That old man was right, you know."

"About what?" I keep my face steady as my heart thumps. I know exactly what he's talking about.

"About my father falling apart when my mother left."

A lump forms in my throat. The controversy between the King and former Queen rocked the Kingdom when it happened all those years ago. The former Queen had an affair with the King's brother, and the two of them ran off together.

After that, the King fell into a depression. He isolated himself, and the economy started falling apart. Trade deals faltered. The people of Argyle suffered.

"What happened, exactly?" My voice is small.

"Pretty much what the newspapers said. My mother cheated, and it broke my father's heart. After she left, I think he had no interest in ruling anymore. It all became too much for him."

"Maybe it's better to go into it alone," I say softly. "Becoming King without a Queen means you can't get hurt."

"I used to think that," Theo says, meeting my eye. "I'm not so sure anymore."

The lump in my throat turns into a massive boulder. It's hard to swallow, let alone speak. Our hands are still interlaced, and I'm worried that Theo can feel the violence of my heart banging against my ribcage.

"I don't know if I can do it alone, Cara." His voice is soft, and his eyes are full of pain. "My father will step down soon. He has to. Once that happens, who can I trust?"

"Your brothers," I answer.

Theo snorts, shaking his head. "Luca might never come back. Dante is content to deal with palace security and stare at computers all day. Beckett still thinks he doesn't belong here. I'm alone, Cara."

"You're not." *You have me.*

The words stay stuck in my throat. The look on Theo's face pierces through my heart as pain shatters across my chest.

I don't ever want to see him in pain. Reaching over to stroke his jaw, I press my lips to his.

"You'll be a great king, Theo."

He gives me a tight smile. "Maybe."

I want to tell him everything in my heart. Everything that has changed over the past week, and everything he's made me realize.

I don't need to leave to feel free. I don't need an adventure. I don't need independence.

Slowly, day by day, hour by hour, Theo is making me realize that the only thing I need is love.

We make love that night. It's different from all the other times, slower and more tender. Theo stares into my eyes, and it feels like there are a million things he wants to say.

There are a million things *I* want to say. Like the fact that I don't want to leave at all. Going to singing school or on some solo international adventure doesn't seem so important anymore. The thought of leaving terrifies me, but not because I'm scared of the big bad world.

Because I'm scared of losing Theo.

For the first time in a long, long time, I feel like somebody *sees* me. Theo sees the real me. He took time out of his busy royal schedule to introduce me to one of our kingdom's best musicians. He knows how important music is to me, and he wanted to show me he cared.

He took me out on the sailboat when he knew I had suffered from Luca's silence.

He understood how much I wanted to leave, and instead of trying to convince me to stay, he took me on this trip to protect me from the pressure that might stop me from going.

No one else treats me like that. No one else sees me like a fully formed human being with thoughts and opinions and feelings. No one else respects me enough to really, truly *see* me.

My mother thinks of me as an investment. My father still acts like I'm four years old and learning to swim with him. My sisters are busy with their own lives and husbands, and they're content to live the life that was set out for them.

As I lie in bed beside the future King of Argyle, I realize that Theo is the only person that has taken the time to get to know me—and he likes me for me. Maybe even more than 'like.' I've seen a different side of Theo. A different side of myself.

The energy changed on that sailboat, and it's grown into something bigger.

Maybe the great tragedy of my life wasn't losing Luca, after all. It's that I'm falling for Theo, even though I have no right to be with him at all.

TWO WEEKS LATER, when we land back at the royal pier on Argyle's main island, a feeling of dread curls in the pit of my stomach. As soon as I step off the sea plane, nausea rises up in my throat. It's the same nausea that has started plaguing my days and nights. I thought I was just apprehensive of this trip coming to an end, but now I'm not so sure.

Stumbling to the edge of the pier, I throw up into the crystalline blue waters.

Theo yelps, rushing over to help me. His broad, warm hand stays on my back as I spit the last of my bile into the water, sucking in a deep breath. My fingers cling to the wooden pier and I squeeze my eyes shut. The nausea subsides and I'm able to inhale again.

I spit the last of my bitter bile into the water, frowning.

That was weird.

"Cara, are you okay?" Theo is still beside me. I turn to see concern written all over his features. Worry is etched into his face like a mask. He helps me to my feet, staring into my eyes. "I'll call the doctor. Come back to the palace with me."

"I'm fine," I say, waving a hand. "It's probably just seasickness."

"You grew up on the sea, Cara. You've been flying in that plane almost every day for the past three weeks. You've never been seasick as long as I've known you. Even when we were being tossed around the ocean on that sailboat for the solstice, you never even got nauseous."

"It's nothing." I try to shrug Theo off, but he won't let go.

"Come back to the palace." His lips flatten—and there it is. That commanding voice that I'm powerless to resist.

Slumping my shoulders, I nod. "Fine."

"Good."

Theo hooks his uninjured arm around my back, his other hand still propped up in a sling.

"I guess the doctor can have a look at your shoulder at the same time." I accept a bottle of water from one of the royal staff with a grateful nod, swishing it around my mouth and spitting it out onto the sand.

How regal of me.

One thing's for sure—I'm definitely not a future Queen. Theo doesn't seem to notice, though. He just stays by my side as we walk down the white, pebbled path toward the palace.

My gut still churns, and an awful taste clings to the back of my throat. Worry snakes its way around the base of my skull. There's one explanation for my nausea that doesn't involve seasickness, but I can't bring myself to think of it right now.

As soon as the word *pregnancy* pops up in my mind, I chase it away. It's too complicated. Too messy. Too permanent.

We walk to the small outbuilding that acts as a medical clinic for the royal family.

Perks of being royalty: on-site doctor visits.

The doctor and nurses take blood and urine samples and runs a few basic tests. I get asked a dozen questions, and by the end of the examination I'm more exhausted than when I started.

I only threw up once. Sure, I've been near the ocean since I was a little girl and basically grew up swimming and running around sailboats, but a bit of seasickness shouldn't warrant this much fuss.

As the doctor examines Theo's shoulder, a nurse pokes her head back into the room.

She clears her throat. "Doctor, could I have a word?"

The doctor grunts, and then helps Theo back into his sling. "Looks good for now, but we'll need at least two more weeks in that sling. You were lucky that nothing tore badly. Should be a quick recovery. Six weeks should do it, and then we can start physical therapy."

The man nods at us, then follows the nurse out the door. I lean back in my chair, sinking into soft cushions as exhaustion settles into my bones.

"I'm fine, Theo. Really. I should just go home."

"So why do you look pale? People don't just puke for no reason, Cara."

I shake my head. "I'm fine. Just need some sleep."

A soft knock on the door tells us the doctor is back. Theo calls him in, and the old man shuffles back through the door with his chin tucked against his chest.

He clears his throat before running his fingers through his hair. The doctor finally raises his eyes to mine, and my stomach drops.

I know what he's going to say before he even speaks a word. Call it female intuition. Call it a premonition. Call it whatever you want.

Before the doctor says a word, I already know I'm pregnant.

17

———

THEO

WHEN THE DOCTOR asks to speak to Cara alone, my heart drops.

Something's wrong. Very wrong.

Cara's face is white as a sheet, and I can sense the tension rippling off her in waves. She meets my eyes, dipping her chin down a fraction of an inch to let me know it's okay.

I clear my throat, wanting to say something. What can I say, though?

Both the doctor and Cara are staring at me, waiting for me to step out of the room. I hover near the door, trying not to eavesdrop but still listening to the muffled sounds of voices on the other side.

The sound of footsteps makes me lift my head. My brother Beckett walks toward me, his trademarked scowl permanently carved into his face.

"Hey, brother," he says. "Or should I say Your Majesty? Not yet, eh? When's the old man stepping down?"

I let out a sigh, reaching out to shake Beckett's hand. He's always had a chip on his shoulder, and I don't understand why. He may be a half-brother, technically—the love-child of

133

my mother and my father's brother—but we've always treated him as family. Even after my mother left with my uncle, there was no question that Beckett should be here with us. He's my brother.

Yet, I've always gotten the sense that deep-seated jealousy is embedded in his heart.

"How was your trip?" I ask, ignoring my brother's question.

Beckett shrugs. "It was fine. Father told me I'd find you here. How's your shoulder?"

"Doctor thinks I'll be able to take the sling off in two weeks."

Beckett grunts. A wicked grin twists his lips. "I'd pay good money to have Cara Shoal dislocate my shoulder," he guffaws, and I tense.

I don't like hearing him speak about Cara like that. Heat flows into my chest. Anger flares inside me, flushing my face and making my ears burn. Protective, animalistic instinct wakes up inside me, lifting its ugly head and staring at Beckett.

He notices.

"What?" He frowns, his lips twisting into an ugly grin. "You don't *care* about her, do you?"

"She's been a friend of the family for years." Somehow, it feels wrong to deny my feelings, even if I'm just talking to my brother.

Beckett arches an eyebrow, smirking. An uncomfortable feeling gurgles in my stomach.

I love my brother. I do. But sometimes, there's something about Beckett that doesn't sit well with me. He always seems like he's holding back. Like he's not telling the whole truth.

When his eyes meet mine, Beckett arches an eyebrow. It's almost like a challenge, daring me to say something.

I ignore it.

Just then, the door opens and the doctor steps through. He bows to me and my brother. "I'd like to follow up with you in three days, Your Highness. We can keep an eye on that shoulder and make sure we get you out of the sling as soon as possible. Excuse me."

With another bow, he walks down the hallway. The door to his examination room opens again, and Cara appears in the doorway.

My stomach bottoms out, and I'm falling through space. How is it possible to get that feeling every time I see her? Like the rug is pulled out from under me anytime she comes into view.

But the ground comes rushing back up toward me when Beckett opens his mouth to speak.

"Cara," he says, taking a step toward her. His voice is low, and his movements predatory.

It takes all my self-control to stop myself from launching at him. I'd tackle him to the ground and pin him there to stop him touching Cara, injured shoulder or not.

But I hold back.

What's going on with me?

Beckett doesn't want to hurt Cara, and I have no right to feel this protective over her. As real as the past three weeks have felt, we're not together. Not really. Soon, she'll be gone.

Her eyes flick to me, full of pain and fear.

I gulp. "Is everything okay? What did the doctor say?"

"Everything's fine. Just need to drink water." Her voice is tight, and I can tell she's not telling me everything.

Beckett glances between Cara and me, his brows drawing together. "Why are you here, Cara?"

"I threw up when I got off the plane."

"The plane?" he repeats.

Cara glances at me, questioning.

I clear my throat. "Cara was with me on the tour of the Kingdom." Beckett's head whips toward me, and I clear my throat. "As a guest," I add.

"A guest." Beckett's eyes darken. It seems the only thing he's capable of doing is repeating everything we say.

"Yes, Beckett, a guest. Do you have a problem with that?" My nerves are frayed. I'm worried about Cara. I'm worried about becoming King. I'm worried about everything that will happen once Cara leaves the palace gates, and if I'll ever see her again once she does.

I don't have the energy to deal with my little brother and the mammoth-sized chip on his shoulder.

"I'll take you home," I say to Cara, extending my hand toward her. She keeps one arm wrapped around her stomach, side-stepping around Beckett. When her other hand slips into mine, I swear I see Beckett vibrating with anger.

Why would he care?

I shake my head, jerking my chin at my brother. "Check in with Dante. He has some updated security protocols for us to go through. You should go and see Father, as well."

"Yes, Your Highness," he says, giving me a low, insolent bow.

I ignore him. Instead, I put my arm around Cara's shoulders and lead her out of the doctor's pavilion. Once we step out into the sunshine, Cara takes a deep breath. It rattles on the way in, and when she exhales, her shoulders drop.

"Are you sure you're okay?" I ask, frowning. My arm stays slung across her shoulders as I hold her close. The royal vehicle is waiting for us, with a new driver standing next to the open door.

"I'm fine. Just need to go home and get some sleep."

I nod. A lump forms in my throat, and I'm not quite sure how to respond.

Her home should be here. She should be coming to *my* bed to rest. Cara's place is beside *me*—why doesn't she see that?

When we reach the car, Cara puts her hand on the open door. She turns to me, giving me a pinched smile. "You don't need to come with me. I'm sure you have a lot of work to do at the castle, what with the coronation to plan and all. I'm sure Dante will want to talk to you, too. Hopefully he has some good news for you."

My heart sinks as my stomach twists. It feels like a weight is crushing my chest, making it hard for me to take a full breath. This is goodbye. I know it is, and I knew it was coming. As soon as the sea plane landed back at the main island pier, I knew that Cara would be slipping away like sand through my fingers.

I just didn't expect it to hurt so much.

I clear my throat. "When will you leave on your trip?"

"I don't know. As soon as I feel better, I guess."

"I'm sure you'll want to be going soon."

Cara sucks in a breath and shrugs. "I don't know what I want anymore." Her eyes flick up to mine and her lips drop open, but then she glances at the driver, who's waiting a few feet away from us. Instead of saying anything, she takes a step toward me and lays a soft kiss on my cheek.

"Thank you for a wonderful three weeks, Theo. You've given me so much, and I'm not sure I can ever repay you."

"You don't need to repay me. Having you with me made the whole tour better."

Why is it so hard to speak? It's like a hand is wrapped around my chest, squeezing the air out of my lungs. I can hardly breathe, let alone make words.

"Let me know what Dante says. I'll be in Argyle for a little while longer, and I won't leave until you tell me you don't need me anymore."

Yep, this is definitely goodbye. My chest feels hollow as I struggle to keep my composure. Cara gives me one last sad smile and ducks her head into the car. I close the door behind her and nod to the driver.

Then, I step back and watch Cara Shoal drive away from me. The car rolls down the long driveway and through the tall palace gates, and my heart sinks down, down, down.

I knew our relationship was temporary. I knew I had no right to be with her, or to stand in the way of her plans and dreams. I knew that this was going to come to an end.

I didn't know it would hurt this much to watch her leave.

18

CARA

WHEN I GET BACK to my parents' house after being away for just three weeks, I feel like a completely different person. Before I left, I was convinced that I'd be gone by now. I'd be in Los Angeles or New York or Farcliff. Either that, or stay and be miserable in the life that's been built for me.

Now, I'm not so sure.

I'm carrying Prince Theo's baby. That changes everything.

Leaving seems silly. Staying seems crazy.

How am I supposed to tell Theo? This whole relationship was meant to be temporary. It was a way for me to stay protected from family pressure while he sorted his problems out. A way for me to leave Argyle on a good note. It was a final goodbye to the islands of my youth.

But leaving with a newborn baby on the way? Exploring a new country with an infant in tow?

Insanity.

The royal chauffeur opens the car door for me, and I stare up at my parents' sprawling home. It's the only place I've ever lived. The only home I've ever had. I've memorized every crack and crevice in these walls.

After spending three weeks with Theo, I'm realizing that there's a lot to Argyle that I haven't seen. I want to visit the rest of the world, of course, but my need for adventure was quenched with our tour through the islands.

Maybe Theo himself helped cure my itchy feet.

Thanking the driver, I make my way up the steps toward my childhood home. I push the front door open, listening for noise in the house. It's quiet, except for the distant sounds of the cooks in the kitchen. I slip through the open door, closing it silently behind me.

I need some time to myself to untangle my chaotic thoughts.

Being with Theo *feels* good...but is that enough? Is it enough to feel good with someone for a couple of weeks to then commit to a lifetime with them?

Is committing to him even an option?

Theo and I have never discussed actually being together. We've always operated under the assumption that this would end.

It did end. Approximately fifteen minutes ago.

But with the baby...

Wouldn't that make him reconsider? Wouldn't that make our relationship a lot more real?

Do I want to commit to him and to staying in Argyle?

Committing to being Theo's wife isn't just like anyone else. I'd be giving my life to the Kingdom. I'd be pushing my own dreams aside, once and for all.

My hand drifts to my abdomen, and I think of the life growing inside me. It terrifies me and excites me all at once. There's a sense of wonder that grows with every hour that passes, filling me up like a helium balloon.

Am I fit to be a mother? Would Theo want to be a father?

Could it really work between us?

A thin stream of hope starts snaking its way through my heart. It's a tiny sliver of brightness, but it's there. It's enough to make me hesitate. Enough to make me think that maybe being with Theo is what I really want.

Stay. Have a family. Love a man with all my heart. Serve my Kingdom and find my purpose.

What was my plan, anyway? Run off to the States, maybe to Farcliff, maybe to Paris or London or Madrid. I was ready to leave this life behind and chase my dream of making it as a musician.

But what if I can find myself right here in my home Kingdom? What if I can travel the world with Theo by my side?

I can sing for myself and for my baby. Isn't that enough?

Or maybe, being with Theo would be the final nail in the coffin of my dead dreams. I'd see all these beautiful places around the world and be treated like a Queen, but I'd be sentencing myself to a gilded cage. I wouldn't have the freedom to study music or to sing loud and freely.

With my heart in turmoil, I trudge toward the staircase that leads to my bedroom. Thankfully, the house is silent. My mother must be away with my sisters, and who knows where my father is. Probably in a body of water somewhere, swimming from dawn till dusk. That's where he feels most comfortable.

But just as I think of him, my father appears in the library doorway. His eyes land on me, and I can tell by the shadow on his face that he has something to say. Without a word, he nods to the library door before slipping back through the opening.

I drop my bag at the foot of the stairs and slump my shoulders.

Just when I think life has thrown everything at me, here comes another wave to knock me sideways.

When I enter the library, my father has his back to me. He's leaning on his wide, hardwood desk, with his white-haired head bowed to his chest.

"Close the door."

I bite my lip and do as he says. I'm almost afraid to breathe.

My father is warm and friendly. He's a hugger. He's the one person that I can count on to brighten my darkest days.

But now?

Something's wrong.

He reaches over his desk to grab a yellow legal envelope. Turning to face me, he extends it in my direction. With a trembling hand, I grab the envelope and read my name on the front of it.

The return address is The Juilliard School of Music in New York. I'd applied to their voice program months ago before flying up on a weekend to do an audition. I'd told my parents that I was visiting one of my cousins. I never heard back. I assumed I hadn't gotten in.

My father nods to the envelope, and I tear open the top. My hands tremble and my vision goes blurry as I read the first word: *Congratulations*.

I can't read anything else. My eyes fill with tears and my heart starts racing. I'm lightheaded. I reach for one of the plush chairs in front of my father's desk, sinking into it as I clutch the envelope.

"You applied to music school?" my father asks, sitting on the edge of his desk. His voice is neutral, and I don't have the guts to look at his face.

I nod.

"Without telling us?"

"I knew you wouldn't want me to go." My voice breaks on the last word. I blink my tears away and pull the acceptance letter out of the envelope, forcing myself to read it in its entirety.

It's everything I dreamed of. One sheet of paper, telling me I'm good enough to sing. Good enough to learn at one of the top schools. Good enough to pursue my passion.

"How do you know we wouldn't want you to leave, Cara?"

"You barely let my sisters leave for holidays. After Luca dumped me, Mother wouldn't even let me leave the house. You've had my future planned out for me since I was a little girl. Now, when Theo came here, the only thing that's changed was who I'm supposed to marry."

My father sighs, and I finally force myself to meet his gaze.

The lines on his face seem to have deepened since I last saw him. He runs his hand over his eyes. His rich, dark skin has been weathered by the water and wind and rain, and for the first time in a long time, I see his age.

My father is getting older.

He lifts his eyes to mine and lets out a sigh. "I would never stop you from living your dream, Cara. If this is what you want, you should do it. You should go to music school."

My heart thumps. Did I just hear that right? He's supportive? He wants me to pursue my dreams?

Tristan Shoal is legendary in Argyle for being a hardheaded, determined man. The type of person who wins Olympic gold medals and breaks world records. The type of person who goes down in history books.

He's a hugger, sure. But he's fierce as hell.

I didn't think he'd be the type of man to let me chase my own dreams, especially not when they didn't align with his.

But my father walks toward me, pulls me off the chair and wraps his arms around my body. He crushes me in a hug, and I think I hear him sniffle.

"I'm proud of you, Cara. You'll make a wonderful singer."

My head is spinning. I stare at the crumpled letter of acceptance in my hand that didn't quite survive my father's embrace.

This is what I've always wanted. It's the reason I would sneak out of my house and go to the beach to sing. It's the reason my heart nearly exploded when I met Prudence Halloway.

Singing means everything to me.

But I stare down at my stomach, and I'm not sure that's still the case.

Three weeks ago? I'd already be gone. I'd take my acceptance letter, pack my bags, and say goodbye to my family. I'd be high on life and chasing my wildest dreams. I'd work my ass off to be the best damn singer Argyle had ever seen so I could be right there beside my father in the history books.

Now?

Things have changed. There's a baby growing inside me.

How can I go to music school when I know I'll be a mother in under nine months' time? How can I say goodbye to Theo and choose music over him? Over the baby? Over the Kingdom?

"What's wrong, Cara?" My father chucks my chin. "I thought you'd be happy."

I wipe a tear away and shake my head. "I am happy. Just shocked."

"You look tired. You should get some sleep."

I lift the letter up. "Does Mother know?"

My father pinches his lips, shaking his head. "Not yet. I wanted to talk to you first."

Relief washes over me. I nod, forcing a smile. "Okay. Thanks."

"Hey," my father says with a soft smile. "I always knew

you'd do big things. Luca never deserved you."

I give him a short nod and slip out of the library. Rushing up the stairs, I toss my bag on the floor of my bedroom and lock the door. Flopping down on my bed, I cover my face with my hands and groan.

Just when the choice seemed simple—be with Theo, if he'd have me—life throws me another curveball. I thought I knew what I wanted. I thought I was realizing how much the Prince of Argyle meant to me. The terror of being a mother was starting to fade, and excitement was mounting. I could see a future, bright and hopeful and full of love.

Now, I'm not so sure. With this letter, my dreams are still within reach.

I lift my shirt up to stare at my stomach, wishing I had ultrasound vision to see the little nugget of life growing inside me. I already love it. This baby already has my heart, and I know I'll do my best to provide for it.

I don't want to stifle my baby's gifts like mine were stifled. I don't want to prescribe a life for this child based on what I want for him or her.

Wouldn't attending Juilliard be the perfect example of pursuing something you care about? Wouldn't that set a good example for my child?

As soon as the thought crosses my mind, pain pierces through me and my eyes prickle with tears.

Leaving Argyle means leaving Theo.

I have to choose between my dreams, and the man that I'm falling in love with. The father of my child. The future King of Argyle. The only person that has made me feel valued and important.

Either way, I lose.

The only question is—what am I willing to sacrifice?

My dreams, or my love?

19

THEO

MY BEDROOM IS lonely without Cara. I've gotten used to her company over the past few weeks and being alone seems strange now.

The morning is bright as I wake up in an empty room. I sigh, glancing out the window, and then drag myself out of bed. I make my way down the stairs and out to the beach that hugs the royal grounds. My shoulder feels better than it did a few days ago, and the doctor seemed hopeful that it would heal quickly.

What did he say to Cara, I wonder? There's something she isn't telling me.

When I get to the edge of the beach, I kick off my shoes and let my toes sink into the sand. I inhale the salty sea air and close my eyes for a moment, listening to the sounds of the ocean.

This is my happy place. I love Argyle. I feel privileged to be its future King. I've spent most of my life thinking that would only happen when I was much older, and I'd have my life as my own.

But Father's condition has worsened, and I need to step up.

After my trip with Cara, I'm starting to feel ready. I can lead this Kingdom. I can help turn around the economy and mend the international relationships that my father has allowed to wither away. I can try to bring prosperity back to the people of Argyle.

Over the past three weeks, I've started to imagine doing it with Cara by my side. Maybe even a couple of kids running at our feet. It's something I didn't even know I wanted, but now I feel like I can't live without it.

As I walk toward the crashing waves, a seagull squawks above me. I look up at the bird, watching it land a few feet away from me. It cocks its head to the side, as if it wants to ask me a question.

"I don't know, gull. Being the King of Argyle seems a lot easier when Cara is by my side, but I don't know if that's what she wants. She left pretty quickly yesterday."

"Talking to birds now, Doctor Doolittle?" I turn to see my brother Dante walking on the sand toward me. He grins, his shaggy hair blowing in the breeze.

"Birds don't talk back," I grin.

My brother claps me on the back, and I wince at the pain that shoots through my shoulder.

"Sorry," Dante cringes. "I got the final report back from the lawyers this morning. I have news."

"Oh?"

"Turns out, the marriage clause for coronation might not actually be consistent with the laws of Argyle. Every lawyer I've spoken to has agreed. Having a spouse isn't necessary to be crowned King or Queen, according to the law. It's only part of the royal culture. Wouldn't hurt you in a court of law—only in the court of public opinion."

"Is there a difference?" I scoff, shaking my head. "Public opinion is more important than the law."

"Maybe. But you have public opinion on your side. I've been tracking your three-week tour through the Kingdom, and all mentions of you on social media are trending towards the positive."

"How did you do that?"

"I track all the mentions, hashtags, and keywords that come up with your name and variations, and then I run them through a data analysis software to categorize them as positive or negative," Dante explains, letting his eyes drift out to sea. "Then, I crunch the data and get it to spit out overall trends of popularity for you, for Father, and for the government as a whole."

"Of course you do. Nerd."

Dante grins, swinging his gaze back to me. "Someone's got to do it, and I know it's not going to be you."

"I'm hopeless with computers. That's why I let you do it."

"Clearly I got all the brains in the family."

"If my shoulder wasn't injured, I'd be punching you right now," I grin.

Dante snorts before faking a few jabs at me. He drops his arms and lets his lips drift into a smile, nodding at me. "Theo, this is good news. The people love you, and the law doesn't say anything about a spouse. You don't have to marry Cara. You can become King without her."

My smile fades as bitterness coats my throat.

That's supposed to be good news? It doesn't feel good at all.

The past three weeks have been the happiest weeks I've had in a long time. I've let myself imagine what it would be like to have Cara by my side. I've lived in a fantasy-land where everything turns out okay.

But the truth?

The truth is, she doesn't want me. She was only playing along to help me out. If she wanted to stay with me, she wouldn't have left yesterday. She'd have stayed by my side.

"You okay, Theo?" Dante pulls me from my thoughts.

The words are on the tip of my tongue. I want to tell him about these feelings swelling inside me. The fantasy of being with Cara, of living happily ever after.

But I don't know what Cara wants. I don't know if she feels the same way.

I know she enjoyed herself these three weeks. I know she feels happy when she's with me, and that her smile widened and her face brightened over the course of our trip. I know she enjoyed singing with Prudence, and she started thinking of Argyle as a home, and not as a prison.

Is it enough, though?

She'd be giving up her dreams to be with me. She won't have freedom if she becomes Queen. She'll be chained to the duty of being a ruler.

I'm ready for that. I've been preparing my entire life for it. But asking someone else to give up their dreams for the sake of duty... It might be too much.

"Theo?" Dante arches his eyebrows, staring at me.

I shake my head, exhaling. "I'm fine. Just a lot to think about."

"You like her, don't you?"

"Who?"

"Don't 'who' me, Theo. You know who. Cara Shoal. The woman you just spent every waking moment with for the past three and a half weeks."

"Oh. Cara."

"Yes, Cara. The social media analysis didn't just talk about you, you know. Her name was trending in Argyle this week. You two caused quite a splash."

I frown. "What do you mean?"

"Well, looks like your fake relationship was a little too convincing. There are dozens of blogs and videos dissecting every public interaction you've had with her. People are starting rumors that she'll be the future Queen."

My eyes widen. "They are?"

"You need to deal with this, Theo. You can't keep pretending. Father needs to step down, and you need to take the throne whether it's with Cara or without."

"Did your data analysis tell you to say that to me?"

"More or less," Dante grins.

Another seagull squawks above us and comes to land next to the first one. I stare at the two birds and let out a deep sigh.

"What do you guys think?" I ask, then pause for a few seconds. Turning to Dante, I pinch my lips. "They don't know what to do either."

Dante snorts, shaking his head. "Have you told her?"

"Who?"

"Fuck, Theo. Stop playing dumb. You know who. Cara! Have you told her how you feel about her? Have you expressed the feelings that are currently causing you to talk to birds? Have you explained to her that you don't want this to end between you two?"

My heart squeezes painfully. Of course I haven't told her. Last time I saw her, I was telling her good luck and goodbye, and watching her drive away.

How am I supposed to turn around and tell her I love her?

I shake my head. "I haven't told her anything."

"You should."

"Are you the future King, or am I?" I snap. "When did you become so wise? Did you create a data analysis program for giving advice, too?"

Dante chuckles and puts his hand on my shoulder again. He shakes his head. "I'm not wise, Theo. You're just being unbelievably stupid."

20

CARA

I'VE BEEN STARING at my acceptance letter for hours. I barely slept last night. What sleep I did get was punctuated by nightmares.

I stare at the letter. The rest of the envelope contains information about the school and a few pamphlets about the voice program.

As the hours tick by, my decision doesn't become any clearer.

A soft knock on the door makes me lift my head from the paperwork strewn around me.

"Come in!"

Cathy, my eldest sister, walks in. She lifts a cup of coffee and a muffin. "Breakfast."

"Thanks," I smile, shifting to sit up in bed.

Cathy closes the door behind her and gives me a hesitant smile. "I heard about the letter."

"Father told you?"

She nods. "Congratulations. I always knew you'd do big things."

"I'm pregnant." I blurt out the words without thinking, then watch as my sister's eyes grow wide with shock.

"You're *what?*"

"It's Prince Theo's."

"Holy *fuck*, Cara."

I wince. Things must be bad when Cathy is swearing. I think I've heard her say bad words two or three times in my entire life.

She sits on the edge of the bed, placing the coffee and muffin on my bedside table. One of the Juilliard pamphlets crumples beneath her, but neither of us tries to move it. The silence in the room is oppressive. Cathy stares at a spot on the floor, her hands gripping her knees.

"Does Theo know?"

I shake my head. "No."

"When did you find out?"

"Yesterday afternoon, right before I got home."

My sister lets out a long sigh. She runs her fingers over her eyebrows to smooth them, a motion she does whenever she's worried. Finally, Cathy looks at me.

"What are you going to do?"

My bottom lip trembles. I suck in a long breath, and finally force my voice to work. "I don't know."

Cathy's always been the responsible one of all of us. She's the eldest, and she has our mother's strict propriety carved deep into her soul. Her posture is always perfect, and she values things like manners and traditions.

Right now, though, her shoulders soften. She opens her arms toward me and wraps me in a tight hug, rocking back and forth as I struggle to keep my composure.

As the first tears slip from my eyes, I know I've lost that battle. The dam is about to break. An ugly, snorting sob racks through my body, and Cathy just holds me. She rubs my back and shushes me softly until my sobs quiet down and I'm able to pull back.

"I'm scared."

My sister nods.

I breathe in through my teeth, forcing my bottom lip to stop trembling. Finally, I meet my sister's gaze. "I think I love him, Cathy."

"Oh, Cara." Her eyebrows draw together.

"That's not everything."

My sister tilts her head.

"We were only pretending to be together. Theo was getting Prince Dante to look into old laws to see if he could get away with becoming King without marrying anyone." My voice is small when I say the last word. When we decided to pretend to be together, it felt like the right decision. It was just necessity, to keep his father happy for a couple of weeks.

Now, though?

The thought of Theo actively looking for reasons not to marry me breaks my heart. Cracks splinter across my chest as pain rattles through me.

I'm pregnant with his child, and he's trying to find a way to break off our fake engagement.

My life is a mess.

Cathy gathers all the Juilliard paperwork in a big, messy pile and drops it on the floor. I try to hide my shock at my very proper, very tidy sister doing something like that. She climbs into my bed next to me and wraps her arms around my shoulders.

"Come here," she says. "It'll be okay."

Why is it that people always say things will be okay? They say it like it makes a difference. Like I'd actually believe it. How can things possibly turn out okay?

If I go to Juilliard, I lose Theo. I have to raise this baby on my own. Best case, I struggle through voice school with a newborn baby. Worst case, I send my baby back to Argyle while I study—but that doesn't seem like an option to me at all. I already love the little bundle of cells growing inside me. Giving it up to pursue something as frivolous as singing seems wrong.

On the other hand, if I stay, I'm giving up my dreams. No question about it. Once I tell Theo about the baby, I don't even know how he'll react. He's actively looking for reasons not to marry me, and this will just add to the list.

Or maybe, his sense of propriety and duty will force him to marry me for real, whether or not he wants to. That would be the biggest tragedy of all. We'd be sentencing each other to a life of misery, all because of a baby neither of us planned to have.

I already know he doesn't want a wife. I know he doesn't want to lead the Kingdom into the same kind of scandal that happened with his father. I know that he wants to be clear-headed when he becomes King.

Having a wife he never wanted and a child he didn't ask for doesn't exactly fit into that vision. I must have been delusional yesterday, when I thought this baby was actually a good thing. That it might bring us closer together.

"You have to tell him, Cara," Cathy says, resting her chin on top of my head.

"Who?"

Cathy scoffs. "Don't be ridiculous."

I sniffle, chuckling through the last of my tears. I pull away from my sister, leaning against the headboard. "I know."

"The sooner he knows, the sooner you can make decisions. You're keeping the baby?"

"*Yes.*" The word comes out with more vehemence than I intended.

Cathy just nods, as if she wouldn't expect anything else. "So you have to tell him."

"What if he doesn't want it?"

"Then he doesn't deserve it."

Everything seems so simple when my sister says it, but it feels so much more complicated in my heart. Theo rejecting the baby feels like the same thing as Theo rejecting me—and that hurts. A lot.

I don't know when it happened, or how, but I've fallen for Prince Theo. Hard. Harder than I thought was possible. The feelings I have for him are stronger than anything I ever felt for Luca. This isn't duty or arrangement. It's real. It's powerful.

It's going to break me into a million little pieces, and I'm never going to be able to put myself back together again.

Sliding my hand over my stomach, I let out a sigh.

Cathy nudges my shoulder. "Sing me something, Cara."

"What? Why?"

My sister smiles. "Maybe you'll go to voice school. Maybe you won't. Maybe you'll end up with Theo. Maybe you won't. One thing I know for sure, though? You have a beautiful voice and singing brings you joy. Heck, your singing brings *me* joy. It's a gift, Cara. You should use it whether or not you decide to go to Juilliard."

Tears prickle my eyelids, but I try to contain myself. I don't want to cry. I don't want to turn into a blubbering mess and give in to all my worst fears.

Instead, I take a deep breath and I sing the first thing that comes to mind. It's an old love song that Prudence and I sang together, one that our father used to sing to our mother when we were little. Cathy leans against the pillows on my bed and closes her eyes. When I sing the chorus, she joins in with me.

My heart swells.

I haven't heard Cathy sing since we were kids.

She's right. My voice is a gift, and I can't give it up. As a hurricane of emotion blows around me, whistling through the cracks in my armor, I need to cling onto the things that are real.

My baby is real, and I need to protect it. My voice is real, and I need to cherish it.

My love for Theo is real, and I need to find out if he feels the same way.

The door to my room opens, interrupting our singing. My mother stands in the doorway, eyebrow arched. She looks at the pile of paperwork on the floor and then swings her gaze to my sister and me. Cathy shuffles off the bed, adjusting her clothing and clearing her throat.

My mother stares at me with cold, hard eyes. "The Crown Prince is here. He's asking for you."

A MAID PLACES a silver tray beside me. A cup of tea lets off a wisp of steam as the maid curtsies and backs away. My knee bounces up and down. Tristan Shoal stares at me from across the living room.

"We weren't expecting to see you today, Your Highness."

"I was in the neighborhood."

Lie.

I couldn't stay away. I've only been apart from Cara for a day, but after my conversation with Dante, I felt like I had to talk to her.

We're connected. Cara and I share something that I didn't even know was possible. I thought I wanted to be alone. To lead this country to prosperity on my own. To protect myself from the kind of scandal that marred my father's rule.

Now, I'm realizing I was wrong. I don't want that at all.

I want Cara.

"Cara got some good news in the mail," Tristan says, reaching for his own cup. It looks tiny in his meaty hands. Even as he ages, he looks like an athlete. Still a national treasure, and now the terrifyingly imposing father of the woman I'm falling in love with.

"Did she?"

Tristan nods, a proud smile tugging at his lips. "She was accepted to The Juilliard School in New York. To study singing." His eyes gleam, and my heart stops dead. If Tristan notices, he doesn't let on. "I always knew she had a gift."

"N-New York?" I repeat.

Tristan shifts his gaze to me, nodding. "I was shocked, too. I think people like you and me—who have the soul of Argyle deep in our bones—don't understand wanting to leave this place. It's paradise."

My throat is tight. I nod.

"But Cara's different." Tristan smiles again, sipping his tea. "She's always wanted to see the world. To be independent. I didn't understand it until she got that letter in the mail. Now, I know. She wasn't meant to be held down. She's like a bird. She needs her freedom."

Another Doctor Doolittle. Great.

I rack my brain to try to think of something to say, but all I can think of is Cara leaving.

She doesn't feel what I feel. She doesn't want to stay. She doesn't want to see if things could work between us.

Her father's words hit me like a sledgehammer to the gut, because I know there's truth to what he's saying. Cara *does* need her freedom. She deserves to explore the way she's always dreamed. She should go to the best voice school in the world to pursue her dreams.

Who am I to hold her back?

Keeping her in Argyle, no matter how much she thinks she cares about me, would be wrong.

As the realization settles in, my heart sinks deeper and deeper, until I'm not sure it's even part of my body at all.

Then, Cara appears in the living room doorway. I stand up, staring at her makeup-free face and her red-tipped nose. Her eyes are clear, and she stares at me with a million questions in her eyes.

Pain shatters through my chest.

I need to let her go. As soon as I see her face, I know Cara deserves to be set free. If she stayed, I'd be condemning her to a life of duty. Of service. Of living in the public eye.

A life without singing, unless it was in the privacy of our own home.

She'd never be able to share her gift. She'd never be able to study music. She'd never be able to explore the world the way she wants to.

Cara sinks down into a curtsy, and the movement makes a lump appear in my throat. It's too formal for how I feel about her. She shouldn't be curtsying for me. She should be running to me and throwing her arms around my neck. She should be planting a kiss on my lips and smiling at me, pressing her body into mine.

But the distance between us grows. She stands up straight, moving to sit beside her father.

"I wasn't expecting you tonight, Th— Your Highness."

I wince at the formal title. Twenty-four hours ago, before we flew back to the main island, I had my face buried between her legs. Now she's talking to me like she doesn't even know me.

"I was hoping to speak to you alone." I glance at her father, whose eyes narrow ever so slightly.

There's a slight pause, and then he heaves himself off the sofa. "I'll leave you to it."

We watch him walk away. I stand up, moving to sit next to her. "I heard about your acceptance to Juilliard," I start.

Cara's eyebrows jump up. She glances at the door where

her father disappeared, then lets out a sigh. Her hand moves to her stomach as she shifts her gaze back to me.

"I only heard about it yesterday when I got back."

"Congratulations." My voice is flat.

"Thank you." Her eyes are dim.

Silence settles between us, and I try to find the right words. If I tell her I'm falling for her, will she feel obligated to stay? To give up her dreams? To sacrifice everything she wants just for me? Will I only be making her decision to leave that much harder?

Maybe I shouldn't tell her anything. Let her leave without looking back, just like she wanted.

I take a deep breath. "I spoke to Dante."

"Oh? Did he find anything?"

I nod. "Apparently having a spouse is only convention, not law. He thinks that with public opinion of me being so high, I can probably take the throne without getting married."

Cara swallows. She forces a smile that doesn't quite reach her eyes. "That's good news."

"Is it?"

She doesn't answer.

"I haven't spoken to my father yet," I continue. "But if you agree, I'll tell him that the engagement is off. That I'm not taking a wife before the coronation. That you're pursuing your dreams in New York."

Cara's eyes fill with tears, but she blinks them away rapidly. She clears her throat. "If that's what you want, it sounds good. Logical."

"Is it what you want?"

"Does that matter?" Her gaze sharpens. She tilts her head as her hand stays on her stomach. It's like Cara's wrapping her arms protectively around herself, and I hate that I have that effect on her.

"Of course it matters."

"Theo, you're the King. You're the one who needed a wife, and I'm the one who agreed to pretend. Why do you care what I think?"

"Because I care about you, Cara."

She frowns, scoffing. "Are you asking me if I want to marry you?"

I gulp. "I don't know. I'm asking you what you want."

"Why?"

I jab my fingers through my hair. This is going all wrong. Nothing is coming out the way I meant it to. I wanted to come here, profess my love for her, and find out if she felt the same way. I had visions of her throwing her arms around me and promising herself to me. Saying she wanted to be my wife. Telling me she wanted to have my children.

But her acceptance to voice school changes that.

Now, if I tell her how I feel, I'm standing in the way of her and her dreams. Asking her to give up singing school is too much of a sacrifice. She'd be giving everything up...for what? For me?

I take a deep breath. "I care about you, Cara. I just want you to be happy."

Cara's face crumples as she turns away from me.

"Cara..." I put my hand on her thigh, the heat of her body sending a zing of heat through my arm.

Can I really let her go?

"Cara, I'm so proud of you. You deserve to go to the best voice school. You're going to do amazing things."

When she turns to face me, her eyes are clear again. She takes a shaking breath, gulping.

"So I guess this is goodbye?"

My heart squeezes. "I guess so."

When Cara leans over and presses her lips to mine, I know it's over. My heart splinters and cracks, sending pain radiating through my chest. Agony shoots through every muscle, every bone, every ligament and tendon in my body. I tremble, leaning my forehead against hers as I suck in a painful breath. My shoulder aches. Everything hurts.

Cara pulls away first, not meeting my eye.

"You'll make a great King, Theo." She stands up, smoothing her shirt down before lifting her gaze to meet mine. "Thank you for taking me with you on the tour. Even though it was temporary, it was one of the best experiences I've had in a long time. Maybe ever."

So, stay. Be with me. Marry me. Be my queen.

The words are trapped in my chest. I stand up, bow, and turn on my heels to walk away.

Cara doesn't follow, and I show myself out of her house. It's done.

22

CARA

WHEN I WALK OUT of the living room, Cathy is standing near the doorway. Her lips are pinched and her eyes are full of sadness.

Behind her, my mother is leaning against the wall.

"What are you thinking, Cara?" my mother chides. "Did you just turn down the Crown Prince?"

"I can't turn down someone who's not asking me to be with him."

"Oh, please," she answers, rolling her eyes. "I couldn't hear everything, but I know what the look on his face meant."

"You shouldn't have been eavesdropping."

I turn away from the two of them, unable to withstand the assault of their gaze. Cathy looks heartbroken. She knows I didn't tell Theo about the baby.

In my mother's eyes, all I see is disappointment and deep-seated anger. I just ruined all her hard work. All the years she spent moving up the social ladder in Argyle. All the money she spent clothing us and sending us to etiquette school. All the social events she attended in order to get us closer to the royal family.

I finally had the chance to make it all worthwhile, and I threw it away.

At least, that's what my mother thinks.

I could see Theo's eyes. I heard him with my own ears when he told me about Dante's discovery. Even if we had a magical few weeks together, that's all it is—a few weeks.

I can't marry him. I can't become Queen of Argyle. It's not what Theo wants.

He wants to be a good king, and serve the people of Argyle. He wants to be responsible and dutiful, and being with me isn't part of his plan. Having a baby isn't part of his plan.

All we've done is confuse each other, and it's over now.

I would say it's simpler this way, but I have a baby to deal with.

Shrugging away from my mother and sister, I head up to my bedroom. As soon as I close the door, I lean against it and shut my eyes. A deep, painful sigh slips through my lips.

I won't cry. I can't. I need to be strong.

If Prince Theo wanted to be with me, he would have said so. He wouldn't have waffled on about me being happy. He wouldn't have said anything about Juilliard, or about the laws allowing him to become King.

He would have said he loved me. He would have told me he'd die without me. That he needed me by his side. That he wanted me. He would have made it easier for me to tell him about the baby, because I'd have known I was safe in his arms.

But he didn't. He basically told me to leave, and then showed himself out.

My head is a mess. My heart is broken. I'm pregnant, and alone, and about to face the wrath of my mother.

The pile of Juilliard paperwork is still scattered on the floor next to my bed. I move over to it, picking up the sheets of paper one by one. When I pick up the letter of acceptance, I let out a shaky breath.

As I read the words for the thousandth time, I know what I need to do. There's only one option open to me now. Theo made that clear.

I need to go.

I have to show my baby that it's important to pursue your dreams. I have to be independent and chase something bigger and better than Argyle.

A tear slides down my cheek when I think about what that means.

It means saying goodbye to Theo. For good.

But isn't that what we just did?

I sink down onto my bed and finally allow myself to cry.

FOR THE NEXT WEEK, I avoid everyone. Especially my mother. That's two relationships with two princes that I've ruined, and she's not happy about it.

Maybe I should look at the signs that are staring me right in the face—it's not meant to be.

My saving grace is my father. He books me a flight to New York and finds me an apartment close to The Juilliard School. He wraps his arms around me and tells me he's proud of me.

I don't have the heart to tell him about the baby.

Maybe once I'm out of Argyle and away from my suffocating family, everything will make more sense. I'll be able to clear my head.

One week after I say goodbye to Theo, I board a plane from Argyle to New York City and I say goodbye to my old life. I clutch my belly, knowing that I only have a couple of months before my pregnancy starts to show. There's a time limit to my silence. An expiration date to my secrets.

Soon, everyone will know, whether I say it or not.

As the plane takes off, I know I need to tell Theo before that happens. Cathy's right. The future King deserves to know. If rumors and secrets start being exposed, it'll hurt him. I don't want that.

Now that I'm leaving, though, I can't tell him in person. Calling seems too difficult. Texting is cowardly. I watch the runway shrink below the plane, and I leave my heart behind.

What would I even say? How can I overcome all the obstacles and lies that we've told ourselves—and each other?

When the plane is in the air, I pull out a spiral-bound notebook from my carry-on bag and start drafting a letter of all the things I didn't have the courage to tell him face-to-face. I don't know if I'll send it. I might burn the letter as soon as we land—but I need to write it. I need to get the words out.

I tell him I care about him. The weeks we spent together were the happiest weeks of my life, and I think he'll be a wonderful King. He showed me a side of life that I didn't know existed—one full of laughter and love and happiness. When he brought me to see Prudence, he reignited my love for singing and made me believe in myself again.

He gave me my voice back, and even though he encouraged me to leave, I never wanted to go at all.

Finally, I tell him I'm carrying his child. My hand trembles when I write the words, and a teardrop smudges the ink from my pen.

It feels good to write it down.

By the time I'm finished writing, my cheeks are wet with tears and it feels like a weight has been lifted off my shoulders. It's cathartic to write the words, even if he hasn't seen them yet. I read the letter over as my bottom lip trembles, and all the emotion of the past couple of weeks swells inside me.

Do I really want to send this? Will it only make things worse?

I know Theo is a dutiful person. If he sees that I'm carrying his child, will he feel forced to come make an honest woman out of me? Will he be afraid of the scandal? Will it change anything at all?

The seatbelt sign turns on, and the flight crew announces that we're starting our descent. I look at the letter on my notebook for a moment before closing the cover and tucking it away. The landing is bumpy, and I grip the armrests until my knuckles turn white. When we finally come to a stop, my heart is thumping and a thin sheen of sweat covers my body.

I don't know if it's the fear that spiked my veins during the landing, or the relief of making it through alive, but as soon as I get off the plane I feel like a new woman. I go through customs and immigration in a daze, feeling the weight of my notebook in my bag as if it's dragging me down.

Then, like a beacon of light in a dark night, I see a kiosk. The United States Postal Service logo calls out to me from across the airport lobby.

Without hesitation, I stride toward the kiosk. I drop my bag at my feet and rip it open, hunting for my notebook. I tear the scribbled pages out of it, ignoring the ragged edge of the paper. I stuff my words in an envelope and glue it shut, then scribble Prince Theo's name on the front, then hesitate.

If I send it to the palace, will someone else read it? There's tight security on mail that enters the palace. Not everything makes it to the royal family, and I don't trust the workers to keep my secret. No one can know about this baby except for Theo.

Instead, I mark down the P.O. box that Luca and I used to

use to communicate. The one I checked every single day. The one that was always empty, slicing my heart over and over like a thousand little paper cuts.

I hand the letter to the USPS worker and pay the few dollars needed to send it.

As soon as the letter slips through the slot, I let out a breath.

I don't know if he'll receive it. Does anyone even check that P.O. box anymore? Or was that letterbox just a monument to my desperation?

Staring at the slot where the letter disappeared, I realize that it doesn't matter. What felt good about that was telling the truth. It was owning up to my feelings and putting them into words. Once they were on the page, they became real.

Next time I visit my family, I'll check the P.O. box. If the letter is still there, I'll know that Theo was never meant to know the truth of my feelings.

If he receives the letter and reads it, I'll find out how he feels. His actions will show me. He'll either accept me and the baby, or he'll turn me away. Either way, it's out of my hands now, and that feels good. I've done what I can do. It's up to Fate to do the rest.

I walk away from the USPS kiosk with my head held high and a lightness in my heart. For the first time since this whole mess with Theo started, I've been honest.

I told the truth.

I love Prince Theo. I'm carrying his child. I'm not sure about being in New York, but I don't want to stand in the way of Theo being the King that Argyle deserves.

I'm not asking anything of him, and I'm not promising anything of myself. We're in different countries now, and we've decided to walk separate paths. Writing that letter and slipping it through the mail slot was my final act of courage.

The simple, naked truth is all I wrote, and it's all that matters.

Now, I can move on.

23

THEO

THE DAY CARA LEAVES ARGYLE, a gray, driving rain soaks the island. I stare out of the window in my palace bedroom, watching the waves crash onto the shore of the royal beach. Palm trees bend and wave in the heavy winds, their trunks arching so much it's a miracle they don't snap.

I turn away from the window when someone clears their throat behind me. My father stands in the doorway, his hand gripping a cane. I motion to a nearby armchair. My father groans as he sits down, letting out a long sigh as he settles into the chair.

"So," he says. "You never intended to marry Cara Shoal at all."

I grimace and shake my head. "No."

"Why didn't you just tell me?"

"You're not exactly easy to talk to when you get an idea in your head."

My father leans the cane on the side of the armchair before interlacing his fingers in front of his chest. He leans back, breathing slowly. I take a seat in the armchair opposite his, crossing my leg over my ankle.

173

We have surprisingly few quiet moments like this one. Even with my father's illness progressing, there's always hustle and bustle near the King. He's always needed by half a dozen people.

Right now, though, we're alone.

He nods to my shoulder. "When do you take the sling off?"

"Doctor says I should be okay to take it off in a week."

"Quick recovery."

"Six weeks," I answer, thinking back to that day on the sailboat when Cara saved my life. That was the start of a chain of events that I could never have anticipated. A whirlwind of emotion and happiness that I thought would never happen to me.

Then, a deep, dark sadness that I'm not sure I'll recover from.

My father grunts. "Once the sling is off, we can proceed with the coronation."

"So soon?"

"Well, we don't need to wait for a wedding now. Might as well make you King."

"Are you sure you want to step down?"

My father chuckles, then spreads his hands out. "Look at me, Theo. I'm a decrepit old man. I can hardly walk, and every movement pains me. You think I can sort through stacks of paperwork every day? Reading more than two lines makes my eyes sore." He sighs, shaking his head. "I'm not being fair to Argyle and her people. It's time for you to step up."

My father shifts his weight as if to get up when I stop him. He glances at me, eyebrows arched.

"Father," I start, hesitating. I take a deep breath. "Why were you so insistent on me getting married when your marriage ended in such disaster? I saw the way you changed after Mother left. Why would you push me toward something that hurt you so much? I thought you, of all people, would be supportive of me becoming a bachelor King."

My voice is gravelly. It's hard to get the words out, and once I speak them, I regret them. I shouldn't be dredging up the past.

But my father leans back in the armchair and lets out a sigh. He chuckles bitterly before shrugging. "I don't know, Theo. Even though your mother betrayed me, lied to me, and hurt me, I still sometimes think it was worth it."

I frown, not knowing how to answer. My mother's betrayal broke him. It tore the kingdom apart. We've been in a downward spiral ever since she decided to walk out. Everything from the economy, to our family, to public opinion has suffered.

Father lets out a heavy sigh. "I loved your mother. She meant the world to me." He gulps, staring off at something over my shoulder. "Even though she hurt me, having her by my side was a gift. She gave me you and your brothers."

My father's eyes flick back to mine, shining with unshed tears.

A lump forms in my throat. That's the most emotion the King has shown since my mother walked out. It's the most fatherly thing he's said to me in many years—maybe ever.

"Are you sure you want to do this alone?" he asks softly.

"Become King?"

My father nods. "It's a heavy burden to bear."

I suck a breath in through my teeth, not quite knowing how to answer.

The truth?

Absolutely not. I want to jump on an airplane and drag Cara back to me. I want to watch her walk down the aisle toward me with a glowing smile on her face and then promise to spend my life with her. I want to have her by my side, supporting me. Being my Queen. Carrying my future children. Making my life complete.

But those are things that *I* want. Bringing Cara back is asking her to sacrifice everything she's ever dreamed of. It's asking her to change her life plans to be with me, when five weeks ago, she didn't even think she'd speak to me again. It's asking her to hurt Luca. Even though he pushed her away and made her suffer, I know Cara would hate to cause him more pain.

As much as I want Cara beside me, I can't ask that much of her. I can't ask her to give everything up to be with me. I can't make her change her dreams just to support me in mine.

What's that thing people say? If you love someone, you have to let them go.

I never knew what that meant until now. I love Cara. In the depths of my heart, past all the jagged edges and broken pieces, there's a warm spot carved out for her. I love her fully, completely, and eternally.

And that's exactly why I can't ask her to marry me.

My eyes flick back to my father. I nod. "I want to do it alone."

Heaving himself off the armchair, my father hobbles toward me and pats my shoulder. "You'll be a good king, Theo. Time to make you one."

THE DAYS DRAG ON. The next two weeks are spent in preparation for my coronation. It's announced to the Kingdom, and the mood in the streets is jubilant. Dante and Beckett congratulate me, and my father seems to relax.

I made the right decision. Wearing the crown is what I was born to do.

Loving Cara doesn't change that. Being King is a lonely life sentence, and I've known that since I was a child.

When my sling comes off, the doctor checks me over and nods in approval. "Good. You'll need regular physical therapy, but there doesn't seem to be any permanent damage. Your range of motion will be limited for now. Try not to do any heavy lifting. We can start your physical therapy tomorrow."

"Thanks, Doc."

"How's your lady-friend doing? I thought I'd be seeing her again."

I frown. "You did? Is she okay?"

The doctor's eyebrows twitch ever so slightly upward. He clears his throat before nodding. "She should be fine, Your Highness. Excuse me." He bows and retreats out of the room.

A wave of nausea rises up inside me as fear rattles my chest.

Is there something Cara isn't telling me? Why would the doctor think he'd be seeing her again?

Before I can spiral into my own thoughts, Dante appears in the doorway. My brother smiles at me, nodding to my shoulder.

"All fixed?"

"More or less."

"Fixed enough to wear a ceremonial uniform and get a crown placed on your head?"

I grin, nodding. "I'll manage."

He has a tablet tucked under his arm and turns the screen toward me. "Here's the security plan for the coronation. I've updated the software for the security cameras and had the chief of security put extra staff on. As you know, you'll have to appear at the palace balcony. We're expecting a couple thousand people to show up."

"I'm not afraid of the public, Dante. I've been walking among them for years."

My brother looks at me, frowning. "Theo, you're going to be the King of Argyle. *Everything* is going to be different." He holds my gaze for a few seconds, and then places the tablet on my desk. "Have a look through the plan and let me know if you want me to change anything."

I nod, unable to speak. His words hit me like a slap across the face.

Everything will be different.

Everything.

I'm no longer Theo, Prince of Argyle. I'm no longer free to go on solstice sailboat trips around the islands. I'm no longer able to take Cara to hidden villas and visit old soul singers. I'm about to be a king with no queen. A man at the helm of this kingdom with no one to rely on except myself.

As my brother walks out of my room, I let out a heavy sigh.

I love her, and I let her go.

That was my first act as King of Argyle. My first selfless decision. The first truly good thing I've done, and the beginning of a long, difficult lifetime as the ruler of Argyle.

24

CARA

NEW YORK IS MUGGY. I miss the fresh, clean air of Argyle, and the soft sea breeze that sweeps over the entire Kingdom. Instead, my days are filled with smells of smog, car exhaust, and warm garbage.

It's been two weeks since I arrived. Two weeks since I mailed the letter. Two weeks since I made the decision to leave Theo behind.

My semester at Juilliard doesn't start for another three weeks, at the beginning of September, but I've enrolled in a prep class to get myself up to speed. I've taken very few voice lessons in my life, so I figured having a couple of weeks of formal training before the official start of the semester would calm my nerves. My teacher is a stern, black-haired woman in her fifties. She has a sharp nose and thin lips, and always makes me feel like I'm doing something wrong.

By the end of my first week, I'm dreading my lessons and wondering if this is what I really want. There's no joy in singing here. No soul. It's cold and technical, without the love and warmth that I expect from music.

After a grueling hour with Miss Dorothea, I trudge

through the busy streets and make my way back to the apartment that my father arranged for me.

It's small. When I look out the window, all I see is another brick facade.

I miss the ocean. It's pathetic how homesick I feel. Slumping down on my sofa, I lean back and wonder for the millionth time if this was all a mistake.

Then my phone dings, and I see an unfamiliar number on the screen.

Unknown number: Hi Cara, it's Jordan. We met at Miss Dorothea's studio. I was wondering if you were free tonight? My friend's band is playing at a bar and I've got no one to go with.

I stare at the message, reading it and re-reading it. Is that...a date? I remember Jordan. We met on my first day and I've seen him a couple of times since. He's got long, dark hair that falls to his shoulders. Most days, he wears it in a low bun. He's handsome, in an artsy sort of way. Like a tortured singer who loves nothing more than to make you melt with his voice.

He wants to go out with me?

It feels wrong. I don't want to go out with Jordan, no matter how angelic his voice is.

But as I listen to the honking cars outside and inhale another lungful of stale air, I know I need to get out. The only way I'll survive in this city is if I make friends and shake off this homesickness.

I type out a quick answer and then jump in the shower to get ready. My stomach twists into knots, and my thoughts fly to Theo.

I don't want to go out with another man, but I do want to get out of this tiny shoebox apartment. Maybe I can just be clear with Jordan that I only want to be friends. I can go out, listen to music, and forget about the oppressive sadness that clings to my every pore.

A couple of hours later, I walk into a busy, dimly-lit bar. The band is already playing, and I spot Jordan sitting at a worn, wooden table. His eyes meet mine, and he raises a hand. A brilliant smile flashes across his face.

He really *is* very good looking, objectively speaking. Not in the makes-my-body-burn kind of way, but I can appreciate his particular brand of attractiveness.

When he wraps an arm around me and kisses my cheek, a flush creeps up my neck.

"Drink?" Jordan asks.

Instinctively, I put a hand to my stomach. I shake my head. "Just a seltzer water."

We sit at the bar and listen to the music. Jordan tells me about growing up in New York City with two musicians as parents. He tells me about a show of his coming up and asks me to come along. He tells me a million things, but doesn't ask me anything about myself.

By the end of the evening, I'm drained.

And still homesick.

When I get home, I kick off my shoes and slump down onto my creaky old sofa. I lay back on the scratchy pillows and stare at a jagged crack in the wall, sighing.

Is this homesickness? Or is it my brain and my heart trying to tell me that I made a mistake?

Singing used to bring me joy. It used to invigorate me.

Now, I mostly just feel tired.

And sad.

And nauseous but still somehow hungry—but I think that has more to do with the baby growing inside me than the fact that I'm away from home.

I wonder if my letter made it to Theo. I wonder if he read

it and decided not to answer. Maybe the fact that I left was enough for him to walk away, whether or not I'm carrying his child.

Picking up my phone, I type his name into a search engine. My eyes widen when I see news of his coronation. I didn't even know it was happening today. I click on a video and watch the news coverage of the ceremony. My heart squeezes when I see his face on the screen, and I hold my phone just inches from my nose.

A tear leaks out of my eye, and I brush it away.

I have no right to be sad about this. I left. I said goodbye. I chose New York over Argyle. Myself over him. My dreams over his duty.

I was never meant to be Queen.

This is for the best. It's what I wanted.

...Right?

The video cuts to Theo on the palace balcony, with his father by his side and his brothers standing behind him. This time, I don't brush my tears away.

He looks regal. Strong. He smiles, waving to the thousands of Argylians that have gathered at the palace gates to greet their new king. My heart aches at the thought that I could have been there beside him.

Turning my phone's screen off, I toss it aside and sob into my hands.

In the silence of my tiny apartment, as the crowd's cheers are still ringing in my ears, I know I've made a mistake. I should have told him how I felt. I should have gotten over my own stupid pride and my misplaced desire to be independent.

I should have realized the thing that was smacking me in the face: I'm in love with Theo. Desperately. Hopelessly.

I love him more than I could have imagined. It burns a

hole right through my chest, sending daggers of pain through to my fingers and toes.

Is love supposed to hurt this much?

My sobs turn to trembling whimpers, and I lay on the couch in the fetal position. I wrap my arms around my stomach and squeeze my eyes shut.

Theo is King now. That in itself is like the final nail in the coffin. I'm nothing but an aspiring singer. The youngest daughter of an Olympian and a wannabe socialite who failed to live up to her parents' expectations of marrying well.

But none of that matters. I don't want to be Queen.

I just want to be with Theo.

As I stare at the brick wall outside my window, exhaustion settles into my spirit. Theo has other responsibilities, and the flame of our love affair has died out. My hands curl around my belly, and I turn my thoughts to my baby.

Maybe, this child is the most precious gift Theo could have given me. It's a piece of him. A piece of his love. A piece of the pure happiness that I felt while on tour with him.

My baby is a reminder that even though things come at a cost, there are beautiful things in the world.

I dry my eyes and take a deep, shaking breath.

Theo might be out of reach, but that doesn't mean I can't live a full life.

No matter what happens, I'll cherish this baby like the gift that it is. I'll love Theo from afar, knowing that a small part of him lives on in our child. A child that I get to care for and love with my whole heart. A child that I get to raise and adore. A child that will bring me more adventure than any international trip ever could.

Even through the pain of my heartbreak, I can feel the truth of the sentiment. This baby is everything to me, with or without Theo.

25

THEO

I'M surprised when Luca answers my phone call. His voice is gruff. He's still in Singapore, and based on the reports I'm getting from the doctors, he's doing well. They think he might even walk soon.

Maybe his spirits are up, and that's why he finally decided he wanted to talk to me.

"Congratulations," he says. "You're the King now. Sorry I couldn't be there."

"It's fine. I'm just glad you answered. It's been too long since we spoke last."

A weight lodges itself in the pit of my stomach. He doesn't know that Cara and I had a— What did we have? An affair? A relationship? A fling?

He doesn't know that I spent three blissful weeks with her. He doesn't know that she's gone.

Does he care? He hasn't spoken to her in over a year.

"The doctors seem to think your recovery is going well." My voice is thin. I don't even know how to talk to my own brother anymore.

"They'll have me trying to walk soon. I've been able to

move my toes for a couple of months now. Feeling's coming back to my legs. I've got pins and needles all the time, but I'm too weak to move them. Sick of rolling around in a wheelchair, though."

"Three years is a long time."

Luca grunts in response, and silence settles between us.

"I sent you a card," Luca says after a pause.

"You did?"

"It's not much, just a card and a small gift. You're our new King, after all. Thought I should congratulate you."

"I haven't received it yet."

"I sent it to the P.O. box. Didn't want anyone else getting my address. Can't stand the thought of a surprise visit from Father."

Nodding, I grunt. I'm pacing back and forth in my father's —no, *my*—study. Images of all of Argyle's kings stare back at me, with a bare spot on the wall where my face will soon be hung.

"Haven't checked the P.O. box in months. And you're probably safe on the *visit-from-Father* front. He's weak."

"How weak?"

"Weak enough to make me King."

Luca lets out a dry snort. He sounds flat. Nothing like the vibrant man I used to know. "Check the P.O. box if you want a lame card, then. I don't know why I was expecting you to get it already. I guess you haven't had any reason to look for mail in that P.O. box," he says. "Not since Cara stopped talking to me."

I frown. Luca's voice is bitter. The way he worded that sounds like he partially blames her for the demise of their relationship.

That's not how I see it at all. I witnessed Cara try and try and try to call him, to go visit him, to reach out to him. I saw my brother push her away, and I saw how much it broke her.

I realized too late how much she was suffering. That I hadn't been there for her, either.

Now, she's gone.

Both Luca and I let her go.

It's for the best. I keep telling myself that, but it doesn't make it hurt any less.

"Have you seen Cara lately?" Luca sounds tense.

My heart thuds, and I'm not sure how to answer. Should I tell him what happened between me and Cara? Or would telling him only hurt more? Has he seen the rumors online about me and her?

I take a deep breath and settle on a half-truth. "Not for a couple of weeks. She's left to study singing in New York City."

Luca grunts in response, and a bitter taste coats my mouth. We say our goodbyes, and I let out a deep breath.

That felt wrong, but what am I supposed to say? Cara's gone. She's pursuing her dreams. I'm King of Argyle, and I have responsibilities. Telling Luca about my affair with Cara would only cause more pain. There's no point.

We say goodbye, and I let out a sigh. That felt wrong. I was lying to my brother and to myself.

I square my shoulders and head out the door. The P.O. box is located on the lesser populated side of the island a fifteen-minute walk away. I nod to my personal bodyguard, waving him away, then dodge through the hallways. When I get to my chambers, I grab the tiny key that opens the P.O. box lock, and then head out the door again, praying I won't meet anyone who will have a thousand and one things for me to deal with.

When I get outside, I suck in a deep breath. Fresh air reminds me of being with Cara. It reminds me of feeling the wind in our hair and hearing her laughter skip across the waves toward me. It reminds me of being happy.

I walk quickly, ducking through a side gate of the palace grounds towards the post office box.

This is a fresh start for me and Luca. He's talking to me now. He's asking about Cara. Soon, he'll try walking again. Maybe he's ready to let us in. Maybe, I'll have my brother back and we'll be able to be a family once more.

Cara left, but maybe Luca will come back. It's cold comfort, but it's something.

The post office box stands on the side of the street, out of view of the nearest house. My key slides in the lock, and I open it up. Frowning, I see not one, but two items inside. Luca's package is a small box wrapped in brown paper.

The other envelope is the one that catches my attention. It's from the United States, and the return address is New York City.

My breath comes fast. I'm practically hyperventilating as I tear the edge of the envelope, my hands trembling so hard I slice my finger open. A drop of blood beads on my finger as I swear under my breath, sticking the finger in my mouth for a second to lick the blood away.

When I pull the jagged, ripped pages of a notebook out and see Cara's handwriting, I practically faint. Sitting down right there on the ground next to the P.O. box, I start reading.

My vision blurs when I read about how she cares about me. She feels the same way I do. My heart starts to stutter, and hope flames to life in my heart.

Maybe, maybe, maybe.

Maybe she would come back. Maybe we could be together. Maybe we could live happily-ever-after.

Then, I read something that makes the whole world fall away. In Cara's loopy, slanted handwriting, two words stare back at me. As soon as I read them, I know my life is about to change forever.

I'm pregnant.

I blink, reading it again.

I'm pregnant. It was that first night at the villa when we didn't use protection.

My breath quickens. My heart feels like it's trying to burst out of my chest. My hands tremble as I reach for my phone, and I struggle to dial her number. My hands are too sweaty to get the screen to work, and a new smudge of blood swipes across the screen.

"*Ahhh,*" I whisper-scream at my phone before wiping my hand on my pants and trying again.

I can't see straight as I put the phone to my ear, so I just squeeze my eyes shut. I lean my head on my knees as I sit on the dirt near the post office box, knowing that I make a very pitiful king right about now.

It doesn't matter.

Cara is pregnant with my child. She *left the country* with our baby inside her belly. I pushed her away, thinking it was what's best for her. I told her I didn't want to marry her, when I should have been wrapping my arms around her and never letting go.

The phone beeps, and a robotic female voice speaks to me. The number has been disconnected.

I groan, dropping my head. Of course it's been disconnected. Cara left the country.

As I pick myself up off the ground, I wipe my dirt- and bloodstained pants with equally dirt- and bloodstained hands. Lifting my head up, I stare at the distant walls of the palace and the blue skies beyond. Palm trees wave at me as a soft, warm breeze washes over my skin.

I know what I need to do.

I'm rewriting that old cliché. If you love someone, you don't let her go. You tell her exactly how you feel and beg her to come back to you. You fall to your knees and tell her that you need her desperately, the way you need air, and food, and shelter. You tell her that you want to be a father, a husband, a lover. You tell her that she's your Queen, in every sense of the word.

If you love someone, you beg. You plead. You hold on tight.

You get on a plane and bring her back, and then never let her go.

26

CARA

I HAVE my outfit picked out and my bookbag packed. Tomorrow is the first day of school. The first day of training my voice, developing my instrument, and becoming the kind of singer I've always dreamed of being.

Tomorrow, I take a step toward my dreams.

But are they really my dreams?

These days, it feels more like running away. My real dreams—the ones that wake me up in the night with a smile on my face—take me back to Argyle, to a villa hidden away on a lush, sparsely populated island. Every night, I'm transported back to Theo's arms. Singing doesn't bring me joy anymore. At least, not the type of singing I'm doing here. The thought of exploring the world on my own makes me want to curl up into a little ball and crawl into a hole.

I'm off-balance. He knocked me clean off my feet, and now I'm adrift in the world on my own.

Isn't this what I always wanted to do? To explore? To discover? To see the world?

It doesn't feel right, though. It feels lonely and cold and

stinky. Fear has crept into my heart over the past few weeks, tainting all my decisions.

Is it too late to go home? My father seems to think coming here was the right decision. My mother isn't speaking to me.

Dad doesn't know about the baby, though. No one does, apart from Cathy and the doctor.

My phone buzzes, and Jordan's name flashes on the screen. I sigh. I thought I made it clear that I didn't want anything except friendship with him, but he keeps asking me out. Maybe his intentions are pure? Maybe he wants to be my friend?

Somehow, I doubt that. He has wandering fingers and he always hugs me for a second too long. I always come away from hanging out with him feeling slightly unclean.

I jump when my door rattles on its hinges. Someone is banging on the other side.

Glancing at my phone, I frown.

Is that Jordan? Why would he be here? Is he angry?

Clutching my phone, I take a peek at his message. It just says, *Hey*. No hint of anger. No sign as to why he would be trying to break down my door.

Someone calls out my name from the other side of the door, and I freeze.

Is that...?

It couldn't be.

It's not.

But that voice...

My heart thumps. The banging continues. Whoever is on the other side of that door really, *really* wants me to open.

I tiptoe forward, and the banging stops. I pause, listening for a noise. Something like shuffling, and maybe heavy breathing.

Then, the voice again, as if he's leaning his forehead

against my door. "Cara," he sighs, as if saying my name is the greatest effort. "Are you in there?"

The poor hinges on my front door are taking a beating today. They nearly rip off the wall when I tear the door open.

Theo stumbles forward, catching himself against the doorframe.

"Theo," I breathe, eyes wide. "What are you doing here?"

"I got your letter." He gulps.

"Oh." My heart hammers against my ribcage. Sweat gathers under my armpits as I struggle to swallow. My brain runs circles around me, but still I can't quite manage to say anything else.

"Is it true?" Theo's eyes shine.

I nod. My voice still isn't cooperating.

Theo steps forward, closing the door behind him. We stand a few feet apart, staring at each other with wide eyes. I watch him gulp again, his hands clenching and unclenching.

The air between us is thick. My heart rattles against my ribcage as I can't quite take a full breath. Words still won't come.

He's here, so he must care about the baby...about me.

But the way he's looking at me is making me pause. Neither of us moves. Maybe he's just here out of duty? Maybe he doesn't want me at all?

Worry knots in my stomach as my heart races. My sweating intensifies. I reach up to tuck a strand of hair behind my ear, and my limbs feel heavy.

I shouldn't have told him about the baby. What if the only reason he's here is because he feels he has to be? I'm just another responsibility dumped on his lap.

Theo just stands there as another second ticks by. His tongue slides out to lick his lips, and then he steps toward me.

The tension breaks.

He slides his hand over my waist and pulls me close, using his other hand to cup my cheek.

"Why didn't you tell me?" he whispers, leaning his forehead against mine.

Instead of answering his question, I just wrap my arms around his neck. "Your sling is off." It feels good to have both of his arms wrapped around me.

The Prin—the *King*'s—breath catches, and he closes his eyes for just a moment. "I want you, Cara. I want you beside me, always. I want to be a father to our child. I want to wake up beside you every morning. I feel..." His voice cracks, and I can't take it anymore.

I tilt my head up and brush my lips against his. Gently. Tentatively. Hesitantly.

Theo isn't tentative. He doesn't hesitate. He tightens his hold on my waist and pulls me close, pressing his chest to mine. His lips part as he claims my mouth. He kisses me like never before, showing me exactly how he feels.

My heart flies. I kiss him back, letting go of all my fears and insecurities. I let go of everything that brought me to Juilliard. Everything I thought I wanted.

What I want is love. Acceptance. The freedom to be *me*. I don't want the freedom to run away. I want the freedom to choose.

Theo slides his hand over my cheek, tangling his fingers into my hair. He holds me close, kissing me more fiercely than ever before.

The King of Argyle stands in my tiny, dingy New York apartment, kissing me like there's no one else in the world. His touch feels like heaven. His kiss is all-encompassing. He holds me close, and my world is complete.

Pulling back, the King looks into my eyes.

"Come back to Argyle with me, Cara. Be my wife. Have my child."

I run my fingers over his cheeks and take a shaky breath. I gulp, trying to find the words to say what I'm thinking. This is a whirlwind, and I want to make sure we don't jump into anything. But Theo's looking at me so earnestly, so lovingly, that I'm starting to believe this is real.

I drag my eyes up to his. "I don't want you to feel like you have to do this because of the baby."

Theo's lips tug. His eyes glimmer, and he shakes his head. "Don't be silly, Cara."

"I'm serious. This is a big decision."

"Maybe," he replies. His arm is still slung around my waist, and he sways gently with me in his arms. "But it feels easy. I want to be with you, Cara. The only reason I didn't tell you earlier was because I didn't want to hold you back. I wanted to let you chase your dreams."

"My dreams have changed," I whisper.

"So have mine."

"You don't want to be King alone anymore?"

Theo smiles before kissing my forehead. He lets out a long breath, then shakes his head. "I don't want to do it on my own anymore. I want to do it with you."

My heart expands more and more and more, until it feels like my ribcage is going to explode. The King holds me close and presses his lips to mine, telling me a thousand things without saying a word. His hands explore my body, tugging at my clothing until he splays his palms over my bare back. He slides his hands down to my waistband, groaning as he touches my curves.

His hands are reverent. His kiss is loving. His eyes hold the entire universe, and right now, it belongs to me.

I push his shirt off his shoulders and suck a breath in

through my lips. My heart thumps as my hands skim over his brawn, igniting that familiar heat in my core.

It's a fire that only Theo can light. Heat that only he can create. Energy that flows only when he's near.

And that's how I know that this is real, and it's worth it. Worth changing my dreams for. Worth making decisions I never thought I'd make.

We undress each other slowly, without saying a word. Theo picks me up and wraps my arms around his waist, carrying me to the bedroom. He lays me down on the bed, caging me underneath his broad body.

I nip at his bottom lip, aching for him. Needing him. Wanting to give him everything all over again.

In the back of my mind, as Theo's eyes darken, I wonder if he means it. Does he know what he's signing up for? Is this really what he wants?

Or is he just doing what he's always done—exactly what's expected of him? Is this just another responsibility to him? Another burden?

Theo kisses my lips, my neck, my clavicle. I try to push the thoughts away and mostly manage to do it. I give myself to him, even if it's just for tonight. Even if he's only here out of duty. Even if this happiness budding in my heart will be snatched away all over again.

27

THEO

MAKING love to Cara is the sweetest joy. It makes everything else pale in comparison. Tangled in the bedsheets with her, I know that coming here was the right decision. I couldn't have gone another day without seeing her. Inhaling her. Tasting her. Loving her.

As we lay in bed in post-coital bliss, I trail my fingers over her perfect body. She shivers, smiling.

"That's nice."

Sparks fly from my fingertips to her skin. Goosebumps rise on her skin wherever I touch it, and I know that there's something between us worth cherishing.

"Cara," I say softly.

"Mm?" Her eyes are closed.

"I love you."

When she looks at me, her eyes are misty. A soft smile stretches over her lips, and she reaches over to rake her fingers through my hair.

"I love you too, Theo."

My heart grows. It bangs inside my chest, beating for her. For us. For our love.

"Will you come back with me?"

Cara laughs. "Of course I'll come back with you, Theo."

"What about all this?"

Glancing around the bedroom, Cara arches an eyebrow. She throws her arms behind her head, letting her gaze fall on all the old pieces of furniture in the room. "What, all this luxury?"

"You know what I mean. What about Juilliard? What about singing?"

Cara takes a deep breath. She moves her hand to her stomach, tracing a small circle below her belly button. "I can sing anywhere."

"You can't get this kind of education anywhere. I don't want you to give everything up and then regret it."

Cara looks at me, smiling softly. "When I came here, I already felt like I'd given everything up. Every step that I took away from you felt like a mistake. It tortured me. The thought of being apart hurt more than I could have imagined. The only thing that kept me going was this baby." She spreads her fingers over her stomach. "I knew I had a piece of you inside me."

"I never wanted you to leave. Ever since our solstice sailing trip, it killed me to be apart from you."

Cara smiles softly, shaking her head. "We're just two clueless idiots, aren't we? We can't say what we really feel."

"Watch it," I growl. "You're talking to your liege."

"You going to arrest me?" Cara arches an eyebrow, then cracks a smile. She takes a deep breath, rolling over to place her head on my shoulder. Her fingers explore my chest, trailing back and forth across my pecs. Shivers of pleasure follow her touch, and I kiss the top of her head.

Cara sighs. "I used to feel like staying in Argyle was failure," she says.

"And now you don't?"

"Now, I think the failure is doing something that you feel you have to do. Me coming here, leaving home, doing something that wasn't prescribed—that was just something I felt I had to do for my own pride. When I strip it all away, what do I really want?"

Silence hangs between us.

"I don't know," I whisper. "What do you want?"

Cara lifts her head, smiling. "You," she says simply. "I want you."

WE HEAD BACK to Argyle the next day. I keep checking to make sure Cara's certain. That she knows what she's giving up, and she definitely wants to come back.

Cara's face is radiant, and she just smiles at me. "Theo, stop. This is what I want." Her hand moves to her stomach and her smile widens. She tilts her head, staring at me. "Are you sure this is what *you* want? You're not just doing this because I got pregnant and you feel like you have to?"

Her eyes drill into mine, and I feel like Cara's more serious about that question than she's letting on.

My heart thumps. I nod. "I want this, Cara."

I never thought I wanted children. I've been so convinced that I'm better off on my own and that I didn't want to share my life with anyone.

But now, the thought of having a child with Cara makes the whole world brighter. The rest of my life doesn't seem like a prison of duty to the Crown. Happiness and hope bloom in my heart in a way that I never thought was possible.

With Cara, it's possible. More than possible—it's a reality.

I'm going to marry her and be the father of our children.

As we board the private jet that will take us back to

Argyle, Cara settles into her seat and slips her hand into mine. She leans her head against the headrest, letting a soft smile drift over her face.

"You know, I thought that leaving New York would mean giving up my dreams. That's not what it feels like at all. It feels like leaving behind the old me for something even better."

"What's that?"

"You," she answers, squeezing my hand. "And a new life together." Her smile slips for a second, and she takes a deep breath. "What about Luca?"

I sigh, staring forward as the plane starts to taxi. Cara's hand is still securely in mine, and I'm not letting her go. Not for anything.

"Luca will come around."

"What if he doesn't?"

"He will. He has to. I can't imagine my life without you, Cara. We have a child to take care of now."

"I don't want to be the wedge that comes between you and your brother."

"You're not a wedge between anything. It might take time, but Luca will understand. He pushed you away, and things happen. We have a family now. You're carrying the heir to the throne of Argyle."

Cara sighs, nodding. "Okay."

We fall silent. The plane turns onto the runway, and the pilot starts picking up speed. Within a minute, we're in the air. We leave JFK Airport behind us, cruising through the air toward our home.

Because that's what Argyle is—home. With Cara at my side, Argyle is the only home I want.

Cara stares out the window, and a lump forms in my throat.

I know she's worried about Luca, but there's not much else I can say. I'm not giving her up. Not again. Not for the sake of my brother's pride, when all he did was toss her aside like a used tissue. If he doesn't like the fact that I'm with her, that's his problem.

I just hope Cara sees it that way, too. I hope she believes me when I say that I love her and I want her beside me. I hope she realizes that if I ever have to choose between her and Luca, I'll choose her every time.

As soon as we land, a car is waiting to drive us to the doctor's pavilion near the palace. Cara puts a hand on her stomach, sucking in a breath through her teeth.

"You haven't been to see a doctor since you were here?" I ask.

She shakes her head. "No one even knows about the pregnancy except you, the royal doctor, and Cathy."

When we pull up outside the doctor's office, we're ushered inside immediately. We're taken to the same office as before, and the doctor enters a minute later. He bows to both me and Cara before sitting at his computer and bringing up Cara's file.

"Now, Ms. Shoal, you haven't had a checkup since our initial visit, is that right?"

"That's right. Theo—uh, His Majesty—insisted I come straight here."

The doctor glances at me, and I think I see a hint of approval in his gaze. He nods, tapping a few notes on his computer. "Looks like it's been about seven weeks since the time of conception. It's time to check on this baby. Have you ever had an ultrasound before, Ms. Shoal?"

Cara shakes her head. For the next few minutes, the

doctor explains the process before setting Cara up on a bed. He squeezes some clear gel onto her abdomen before placing a wand on her belly.

Cara's eyes shine, and all I can think about is how badly I want to make her my wife. Visions of a child or three running around the palace grounds with us flood my mind. Cara could teach them to swim, and I'm sure Dante would have them on a computer as soon as they could sit still. They'll be drowned in love from everyone around.

If it's a girl, I know my father will melt. He won't be able to resist a little baby girl. Hell—neither will I.

Excitement and pure, white-hot terror flood through me as the doctor stares at the screen. Fatherhood is a much bigger responsibility than wearing the Crown, but it fills me with so much joy, it's almost indescribable. I hold Cara's hand as if it's the one thing keeping me grounded on earth. If I let go, I might float away into fatherly bliss.

Then, the doctor grunts. His brows draw together, and he slides the transducer over Cara's stomach again.

"Hmm," he says, as if that'll help anything.

"What?" My voice is hard. My heart thumps.

"Nothing to worry about just yet," the doctor says, putting the wand down and calling a nurse. "We'll take a few blood tests and check back in two days."

"Is something wrong?" Cara's eyes have gone from soft happiness to hard, cold fear.

"Usually, at seven weeks, I'd be able to see the embryo via ultrasound. It's unusual not to see it, but we'll run some more tests to make sure everything is normal." He smiles at the two of us, but if he thinks it'll soothe my nerves, he's wrong.

A nurse comes in and helps Cara clean up. I pace the room and the doctor writes notes.

Fantasies of my future children start to crumble before

my very eyes. As much as the doctor smiles, I can tell by the deep lines in his forehead and the curve in his shoulder that he's not telling us everything.

He's worried, and so am I. My happiness with Cara is hanging in the balance, and I already know something's wrong.

28

CARA

Ectopic pregnancy.

I'd never heard those two words before, but now they play on repeat in my brain. There's no room for words, or sentences, or hope, because the only thing I can think about are those two ugly words. Over, and over, and over again.

I took a blood test after my ultrasound, and then another one two days later. That confirmed it.

My pregnancy is non-viable.

Is that language supposed to make it easier? *Non-viable.* Saying it that way is cold. Clinical.

Completely fucking devastating.

There's no room for grief between *non* and *viable*. There's no space for me to understand that everything that has given me strength never even existed at all.

After the doctor confirmed it, he told me I had to have an injection with a drug I couldn't pronounce. Keeping the pregnancy would be extremely dangerous for me. The egg implanted itself in my Fallopian tube, which could rupture if the embryo grows.

I have no choice. I'm confused. Hurt. Destroyed.

I asked for a few days, and the doctor reluctantly agreed. After we got the diagnosis, Theo brought me back to his chambers and sat in a chair, staring at the floor.

After a while, he took a deep breath. "I'd better delay the wedding preparations," he'd said, shattering my heart with six words. Then, he left the room, and I've been alone ever since.

Alone with my non-viable ectopic pregnancy, and the baby that will never be.

Alone with my thoughts that circle around and around and around.

Alone with the crippling thoughts of what's to come.

The injection. The loss.

Is it possible to lose something you never had? I never had this baby. Not really. But in my mind, it was real. It was the one thing that made my life have purpose. It was the one thing that gave me the courage to tell Theo how I felt. It gave me the freedom to let go of my old dreams, and chase after my new ones.

Now what do I have left?

Theo's been gone for over an hour. I don't even know if he wants me anymore. Maybe his whole grand romantic gesture—coming to New York to bring me home, telling me he loved me, saying he wanted our baby—it's all changed now.

If we're not having a baby together, does he still want me? Did he only come and bring me back to Argyle out of duty? Maybe the love he felt for me was only because he knew that I was carrying his child, and he didn't want the controversy to crop up later in his time as King.

Minutes tick by, and my thoughts become more and more bitter.

I gave up everything to come back. My place at Juilliard. My independence. My future.

Now what?

Theo could turn around and tell me he doesn't want me anymore, because I'm no longer the mother of his child. I was a problem before. A potential controversy. A scandal waiting to happen.

Marrying me was a convenient solution.

What happens when the problem disappears? Does he still want me at all?

Why. Isn't. He. Here.

The pillow is soaked with my tears. My face is swollen and my hair is matted. Everything aches, most of all my heart.

I stare at the door in Theo's bedroom, wondering why he left. He wants to delay the wedding. Isn't that a sign of how he feels? He never wanted me at all. I need him to hold me. To kiss my temple and run his fingers through my hair. I need him to show me that he still cares about me. Still loves me.

Finally, I pull myself together. If Theo isn't going to be here with me, I might as well seek out people who care. I need to go home.

I gather a few of my things in my purse and head out the door. A staff member bows to me when I exit Theo's chambers.

"Where's the King?" I ask.

The man bows his head again. "I believe he's in his offices." He gestures down the hall.

With every step, my emotions rage and roil within me. I ask a few other members of staff for directions, finally finding my way to a heavy-looking wooden door. A guard stands outside, lifting his arm to stop me.

"The King asked not to be disturbed."

"He'll want to see me." I cross my arms.

"He was very clear, Miss."

I resist the urge to stomp my feet. "I *promise* you, the King will want you to open this door."

"I'm following direct orders from the King, Miss Shoal," the guard says, his face remaining impassive. "No one is to bother His Majesty."

I try to force my way back, but the guard very carefully puts his hand on my shoulders to stop me. As hard as I struggle, he doesn't budge. I try to shout out, but there's no noise on the other side of the door.

My shoulders drop when I realize the guard will never let me in.

Theo is painfully out of reach, locked in a study and protected by his staff. I'm out here, in the cold, with nothing but my grief and my pain to keep me warm.

I turn around, trudging through the hallways toward the garages. Once there, I ask one of the drivers to take me to my parents' house.

On the way, I text my sisters, knowing that they're busy with their own lives and they probably won't have time for me, either. No one knows I came back. I intended to surprise my family once Theo and I had made preparations.

The result? I'm alone.

As usual.

Yes, I'm wallowing. Allow me that luxury, at least.

When I get to my parents' house, I slip through the front door and make my way up the stairs and into my old bedroom. It's been just over a month since I was here last, and as soon as I cross the threshold, I feel my body start to relax. I collapse onto my bed and curl up in a ball, falling asleep immediately.

. . .

I WAKE up to the weight of a heavy palm on my shoulder. My father brushes a strand of hair off my face when I open my eyes, smiling softly at me.

"I didn't know you were back."

"What time is it?"

"Just after seven o'clock in the evening."

I've been asleep for over three hours. I groan, pulling myself up to sit against my headboard. I rub my eyes, yawning. "I didn't hear anyone when I came in."

My father frowns, staring into my eyes. "Cara, why aren't you in New York? I thought your classes started a couple of days ago."

My lower lip trembles. My eyes mist.

I won't be able to contain the tears too long, but where do I start? How can I tell my father about everything that's happened?

I'd have to tell him about the baby. About how Theo and I thought we were pretending, until it all became too real. How I realized I didn't want to be at Juilliard at all—but now that I'm gone, I don't know where I'm supposed to be.

In a few short weeks, my whole identity became wrapped up in being a mother. I could *feel* the life growing inside me. I knew that this was what I was meant to do.

Now?

I feel like I was kidding myself. My body rebelled against me. I *failed*.

In the process, I got my heart broken and I threw away my chance to be at Juilliard. I successfully ruined every good thing that ever happened to me.

How wonderful. Inspiring. I should write a self-help book. I'm sure my father would approve.

My father swings his legs onto the bed and leans against

the headboard beside me. We sit in silence for a few moments until he takes a deep breath.

"My parents didn't want me to be a swimmer."

I turn to look at him. I never met my grandparents, and Dad never really spoke about them much. "No?" I ask, holding back my tears.

My father shakes his head, scoffing. "No. They wanted me to be a doctor, but I don't know my ass from my elbow. I kept failing my biology classes because I was focusing all my time and energy at the pool. It wasn't until I qualified for the Olympics that they stopped complaining and started acknowledging that I had talent."

I frown. My father has always been a swimmer. Ever since I've known him, he's been a swimmer. Not just 'a' swimmer. *The* swimmer. He's the face of swimming in Argyle. It's his whole life. His business. His identity.

My father lets out a sigh, shaking his head. "When I saw that letter from Juilliard, I knew I was doing the same thing to you that my parents had done to me. I was pushing you toward what *I* wanted you to do, not what you wanted. As soon as I saw that you'd applied to music school, I knew I had to let you go."

My bottom lip trembles, and I can't speak. My throat is too tight.

"Why are you here, Cara?" my father asks gently, nudging me with his huge shoulder. "Why aren't you chasing your dreams?"

I'm afraid to inhale too deeply, because it might turn into a sob. I just take a shaky, shallow breath and then shrug. "Things changed, and I realized I didn't want to be studying there. I don't know what I want now."

"Was it because it was more difficult than you anticipated?"

"It's because I see myself in the people around me. I couldn't relate to anyone. I felt like there was something more important for me to do."

He lets out a long sigh. "You're in love with King Theo."

I turn my head to stare at my father, who chuckles. He shakes his head, sighing. "How does the King feel about you?"

Breathing is still hard. My tears try their best to break past my defenses, but I manage to hold them back for a few more seconds. "Well, I thought he loved me back, but now I'm not so sure."

"No? Because I am. The man loves you."

"How could you possibly know that, Dad?"

"I saw it in his face when I told him you'd been accepted to a music school in New York. Pure devastation written all over his features. I almost felt sorry for him, but I thought you wanted to be up there."

"I did, I think. But it was for all the wrong reasons."

My father sighs. "What do you want now?"

I stare at my stomach, and familiar, ugly words swirl into my head. *Non-viable. Ectopic.*

My father lifts his arm and puts it around my shoulders. He leans his head against mine, squeezing me close. "If that man knows what's good for him, he'll be right here begging you to be with him and have all his children."

And there it is. The sentence that finally makes me burst into tears. Snorting sobs explode out of me as tears flow down my cheeks. Unstoppable. Like a dam bursting, letting the floodwaters gush through.

My father freezes. "Cara? What is it? What did I say?"

I shake my head, wheezing and sobbing and crying so hard I can't see straight. I lean into my father's chest, squeezing my eyes shut in the hope that it'll stop the flow of tears pouring from my eyes. It doesn't help. They keep coming and coming as my father holds me close, saying soft words and stroking my hair until I quiet down.

Finally, I sniffle and stop.

"What's wrong, Cara?" my father says softly. "Tell me."

29

THEO

I HANG up the phone when a commotion starts outside my office door. At least two people shout, and someone manages to bang on the door.

Then, I hear scuffling, and the sound of a very large body landing on the floor.

My head drops. I can't deal with this right now. I've just been on the phone to the staff at the Arlian villa to get it prepared for Cara and me to go. I want to give Cara some time to recover after the doctor gives her the injection, and give us some time alone, away from the public eye.

I need to delay the wedding, which we were rushing to have before the baby started showing. Now, we have time.

And we need to mourn. Preferably together, in private.

I shake my head, not wanting to let my thoughts take me down that dark path. As soon as the doctor told us about the ectopic pregnancy, I've felt like my heart is held together with nothing more than old Scotch tape. A gust of wind could shatter it into a million pieces.

So, I've been doing what I do best. I work. I take care of my responsibilities. I do what needs to be done, if only to stop my mind from spinning back to the visions of the baby that I'll never hold in my arms.

My eyes mist, but I'm pulled from my thoughts by another thump outside my door. Someone grunts, and a female voice yells. It's hard to hear words through the thick, sound-proof door.

"Don't come out, Your Majesty," a guard calls out through the intercom. "Stay inside. We have the suspect under control."

I frown, immediately getting up. When I open my office door, a mammoth of a man is pinned to the ground by three men. Just beyond, another man has his arms around Cara, holding her back.

"Let go of her," I command. The man drops his arms, and Cara stumbles forward.

On the ground, the three guards struggle as the big man bucks. He manages to free one arm, flinging one of the guards across the hallway. The guard slams into the wall with an *oomph*. Plaster crumbles around him.

The other guards shout. One of them presses his knee into the man's neck. Cara screams.

"That's my father!" she cries out. "Get off him!"

In a flash, my hands are on the guards. I pull the guard off Tristan Shoal, letting him stumble to the ground behind me. The other guard gets up, taking a step back. His face is painted in shock.

"We were only trying to help, Your Majesty. These two came barreling in, and—"

"And *what*?" I ask, helping Tristan to his feet.

Not a great entrance for my future father-in-law. He towers over me by a foot, glaring down at everyone around. He bows his head ever so slightly in my direction, his nostrils flaring as anger flows off him in waves.

Cara goes to her father, putting a hand on his arm. "See? Didn't I tell you this was a bad idea? Dad, come on. Let's go home."

"The only bad idea is this sorry excuse of a King turning his back on you," Tristan spits, snarling at me.

"What's going on here?" I ask, holding out my hands. "What do you mean, turning my back on Cara?"

The guards have picked themselves off the ground. Three more guards come jogging around the corner, hands on their holsters. I hold up a hand, stopping them.

"Your Majesty, we apprehended these two as they—"

"Apprehended?" I interject. "Do you have any idea who these two are?"

"They are intruders, Your Maj—"

"Stop." I hold up my hand. "Leave us." I turn to Cara and Tristan, motioning to my office. "Please."

"I'd like to stay here, if it suits you, *Your Majesty*." Tristan spits out my title, sneering as he says it. "I'd like a few witnesses to hear what I have to say."

"*Dad*." Cara steps forward. She puts a hand on her father's chest, shaking her head. "Stop it. This isn't your fight."

"What fight?"

"This piece of shit—" Tristan motions at me, and my guards tense. One of them steps forward until I stop him with a look.

"Dad, stop. Let me deal with this."

"Deal with what? What is going on?" I stare at the carnage around me. A wall sconce is smashed, and one of the walls has a big dent where my guard smashed into it. My team is red-faced and panting, and Tristan looks like he wants to put a hole through me. His shirt is torn at the shoulder, with a thin stream of blood rolling down his arm.

Tristan's chest is still heaving, his eyes flaming. Not the kind of man I like to see angry.

"You have a lot of nerve, asking what's going on," Tristan says darkly. "You leave Cara on her own after she gets news like today. You should be ashamed of yourself, Your Majesty."

"I didn't leave her on her own."

"Dad, please." Cara pulls him away. "Just let me deal with this."

"You didn't deserve the baby." Tristan shakes his head and then turns around. His steps echo in the hall, and his words rattle in my head. Cara turns to face me, her eyes wide.

She gulps, motioning to the office. "Shall we?"

I follow her inside, closing the door behind us. Cara walks to the window and stares out, wringing her hands. I stand near the door, watching her.

"What was that about, Cara?"

"I told him about the pregnancy."

"I thought we agreed—"

"To what? Keep it secret? Let me suffer in silence, alone in your chambers? Is that all you're worried about? How this looks for you?" Her words bite, and I don't know what to say. She shakes her head, tears shining in her eyes. "I thought you might just be doing this out of duty. You might be afraid of the repercussions of an illegitimate child. But I didn't think you'd turn your back on me so quickly."

"Turn my back on you?" I repeat, taking a step toward her. "When did I do that?"

"I can see it in your face, Theo. You don't want me. Maybe you never did."

I jab my fingers through my hair as frustration rises in my chest. My face feels hot. "Cara—"

"The only reason you came to New York is because you thought it was what you were supposed to do. You've always been the kind of guy to do the right thing, Theo, but this is different. I'm not just some responsibility that comes with being King. I'm not some task that you can put on your to-do list and tick it off at the end of the day. I don't want you to be responsible right now. I want you to show me that you care about me."

Cara's chest heaves. Her cheeks are flushed and her eyes shine.

"Cara, is that what you think of me?"

"Why did you walk out of the room after we got the news? Why didn't you hold me, or kiss me? Not even once? I've been up there on my own for hours, Theo. So, yeah. I went to my father. I told him everything that happened. He was the only person who actually gave a fuck."

She spits the last word out before turning away from me. My heart hammers as I struggle to take a deep breath.

How can she think those things about me? How can she believe that I don't care?

"Cara, I didn't leave the room because I don't care about you."

"The first thing you said was that you wanted to delay the wedding." She takes a shaky breath. "If you don't want to do this, just tell me now. Don't lie. Don't drag it out."

I let out a long breath as I squeeze my eyes shut. Then, I take a step toward Cara, wanting to reach out and touch her but being afraid of what she'll do.

"I want you, Cara," I say softly. Her face angles toward me, but she won't meet my eye. I take a deep breath. "I want to marry you. That's the only thing that matters to me right now. I *love* you, Cara."

Her gaze lifts to mine as her bottom lip trembles. "Why were you so worried about delaying the wedding?"

I let out a breath. "I'm sorry. I should have explained. I

just wanted to give you time to recover and time for us grieve properly before having to smile for an army of cameras."

I take another step closer to her, reaching for her hand. She feels cold, and I want to do nothing more than wrap my arms around her and hold her tight—but she's too fragile. She's like a wild animal, staring at me like she doesn't know if she wants to bolt away or rip my head off.

"Cara, I'd marry you right now if I could. You're the only thing that makes sense in the world. I can't imagine being King without you at my side. You're my Queen. Always."

Her lip trembles as a tear spills onto her cheek. I reach up to her face, brushing it away. Cara angles her face toward my hand, sighing.

"I thought you were only marrying me out of duty."

I chuckle bitterly, shaking my head. "No. I'm marrying you because I love you and I can't live without you. I'm delaying the wedding because I need to be with you. Only you. I'm sorry I walked out. I should have explained."

Cara's eyes suddenly snap open, and she shoves my shoulder back. "You need to *talk* to me, Theo. I need you to be there for me, and not just focus on doing the responsible thing. We can delay the wedding tomorrow. Right now..."—her voice is nothing more than a whisper—"I need you."

When Cara slides a hand over her stomach, my heart aches.

She's right. Of course she's right. I pull her into my chest, wrapping my arms around her. I've been so focused on organizing details that need to be taken care of, that I haven't focused on the most important thing. Cara. Grief. Being there for each other.

"I'm sorry," I whisper into her hair. I inhale her scent, feeling the wind pick up that will surely break my heart.

Then, we both break down. Tears come, and don't stop

coming. All the emotion that I've been holding back comes rushing to the forefront. We cry on each other's shoulders, mourning the child that we'll never have.

The Scotch tape flutters away, and I finally allow myself to break. Pain shatters across my chest, radiating through to my toes. Tears flow, and flow, and flow. Grief hits me like a sledgehammer, knocking me sideways.

The only thing that keeps me upright is Cara. She reaches up, cupping my cheeks in her hands. "Don't ever walk away from me again, Theo."

I shake my head. "I won't. I promise."

She takes one of my palms and places it on her stomach, resting her head on my shoulder. We stand in my office, leaning on each other, mourning everything that we almost had.

There's only one thing that pierces through the darkness of that day—Cara. The fact that she's here in my arms. That she's knocked me out of my daze and forced me to stay by her side.

We're together. Still. No matter what.

Always.

30

CARA

WHEN I FIND out that Theo has organized a stay at the villa for the two of us to have some privacy and peace, I shake my head.

"Why didn't you just tell me that you were organizing this? You just ran off after talking about delaying the wedding, and my mind went crazy. I thought you were leaving me."

"I wasn't thinking straight. I kept thinking about the baby —" The King's voice cracks. He swallows thickly, his eyes misting up.

I nod, running my fingers over his scalp and holding his head to my breast. Grief weighs heavy on the two of us. It's an odd sort of mourning. We never met the baby. It was no more than a couple weeks after conception, but the sense of loss is immense. Indescribable.

Heartbreaking.

When the haze lifts ever so slightly, I realize that Theo and I are still in his office, holding each other. He stares at me, tucking a strand of hair behind my ear before kissing my forehead.

"We can try again, Cara," he whispers. "The doctor said we could still have children later."

"Please," I say, shaking my head. "Not yet. Don't say that yet."

Theo nods, wrapping his arms around me to hold me close. We stay like that for an hour or three, I don't know. A long time.

I text my father that everything is okay. Theo and I go for a walk along the royal beach, saying nothing. We don't need to speak a word to know that we're both going through an awful, unexpected kind of heartbreak.

But as the sun goes down and dusk falls, I realize that we still have each other.

Theo might always focus on being responsible. Fulfilling his duty. Doing the right thing.

I might always focus on running away. Being independent. Wanting to be free.

But we balance each other out. He keeps me grounded, and I keep him from burrowing underground.

That day is one of the worst days of my life. It comes and goes, and I wake up next to Theo the next morning with swollen eyes and a scratchy throat.

But I'm here, beside him. He opens his eyes, spreading his arms for me to come snuggle. He nuzzles his head in my hair, groaning in contentment. We lay there, without speaking, knowing we have each other.

We lost something yesterday, but in the light of the morning sun, I realize that we gained something bigger.

I know that Theo loves me. There's no doubt in my mind now. No questions in my heart. Seeing him break down in the office yesterday, and waking up next to him in this plush, feathery bed, I realize that he loves me as desperately as I love him.

He didn't come to New York because he felt like he had to. He didn't ask me to marry him because it was his duty to do it. It wasn't to avoid a scandal or to get ahead of a controversy.

He wants me. Loves me. Cherishes me.

I trail my fingers through his chest hair, inhaling the scent of his skin. It brings a small amount of comfort to my aching heart to know that he is here beside me.

We have many weeks of grief and mourning ahead. I can already feel it coming. But as I lay on Theo's chest, all my doubts disappear. He's here, and he cares about me just as much as I care about him.

THE ROYAL DOCTOR comes with us to Arlian Island. We take the sea plane over, and I still spend the whole ride staring out the window at the crystal-clear waters below.

When we get to the villa, the doctor gives me the injection that will get rid of my ectopic pregnancy. I know he's saving my life. I know it has to be done. I know Theo and I will have other chances to have children, and that in the end, it'll be better to have them after we're married.

I know all these things, but it still hurts like hell. I hold my composure through the procedure, but break down as soon as the doctor leaves the room. Theo holds me, his tears mixing with mine.

Those few days are a haze. I have to get one more injection a couple of days later. I'm nauseous, but I don't know if it's because of the injection or the general heartache and grief that consumes me. Theo is there, always. We spend two weeks in the Arlian villa sleeping, crying, walking on the beach, and generally just recovering from the shock and the loss.

As the days pass, I realize what Theo means to me—and

it's everything. Even more so than before, I realize that he's the one person in my life that loves me for me. He accepts me as I am, flaws and all. He picks me up when I break, and helps me build myself back up again.

They're dark days. I won't pretend they aren't. My emotions are unstable, and it's hard to make sense of what's just happened.

Having Theo beside me helps. The fact that he cleared his schedule to be with me means the world to me, and it shows me that he cares.

Not in a dutiful way. In a real, deep-in-the-bottom-of-his-heart kind of way.

When we head back to the main island, Theo interlaces his fingers with mine. He gives me a tight smile.

"How are you feeling?"

I nod. "I'm okay." It's a lie, mostly. I still feel broken—but I'm not alone. Not anymore. As the sea plane touches down on the water, I take a deep breath and squeeze Theo's hand.

He squeezes back.

The need to run away is gone. The desire to fly off and explore the world is still there, but it's tempered by the fact that I want to do it with Theo. I'm ready to accept my gilded cage, because with Theo, I feel freer than I did before. I never have to face anything on my own. I never have to struggle alone, wondering what I really want out of life.

What I want is Theo. Plain and simple.

Theo leads me away from the palace down a pathway lined with palm trees. A sea breeze rustles through my hair, carrying with it the scent of home. We walk in silence—as we've done most days the past few weeks—until we get to a small gazebo overlooking the ocean.

Theo leads me to a bench in the gazebo and we sit side by

side, watching the waves crash on the white sand. I lean my head on his shoulder as he holds me close, and for just a moment, my turbulent emotions calm down. For the first time since I got the news from the doctor, I feel at peace. I know it won't last forever, that sadness will overwhelm me in the darkest parts of the night—but for now, I'm calm.

Then, the King shifts away from me. He clears his throat, reaching into his pocket for a small jewelry box. Kneeling down in front of me, he gives me a sad smile.

"I haven't done this properly yet," he says, flipping the box open.

A glittering engagement ring stares back at me. My eyes widen as my heart thumps.

"Cara," Theo says, clearing his throat. "We've done everything backward. I haven't been clear or honest about my feelings for you, but I want you to know exactly where I stand. I love you. I want to sit on the throne with you by my side. I want to lead our Kingdom to prosperity together. I want to fall asleep beside you every night and wake up next to you every day."

His eyes shine. My throat is tight, and the tears are already spilling down my cheeks. It feels wrong to be happy about this, when I've been so focused on sadness and grief. But when I nod, unable to speak, Theo slides the ring over my finger with a trembling hand.

We don't say anything about our loss or about what might happen in the future. We don't mention children or heirs or what was or wasn't meant to be. It's not the right time. We just hold each other, kiss each other, and inhale the fresh sea air together.

With a bright thread of hope, Theo stitches my heart back together, piece by piece. I know that we'll come out stronger on the other side. Whatever we have to face, we'll face it together. United. One.

Together, always.

EPILOGUE
CARA

IT TOOK two years to recover from the grief of losing the pregnancy. In that time, Beckett was arrested, Luca forgave me and Theo, and even Dante the hermit found someone to love.

They have their own stories to tell. Our lives were full of twists and turns. Highs and lows.

Before he forgave us, I tried to tell Luca about my love for Theo. I tried to tell him about the baby, and the grief, but his pain was too great. I knew from my own experience that he needed to work through it himself, so I let him be.

And he came back to us. He and Ivy blossomed, and I watched as they gained not one child, but two. Their twins were born healthy and happy. Even Dante and Margot had a child at the same time.

I won't pretend it didn't hurt to see their families grow. I smiled through my pain. Theo stayed by my side, as always. We faced our agony together, and day by day, it grew smaller. It never disappeared, but it became bearable.

Then, like a beacon of hope, I felt new life growing inside me. It wasn't like the first time—chaotic and tumultuous and surprising. This time, we dared to plan it. For the first time in two years, we let ourselves hope. Really, truly hope that we could have a child.

The doctors warned us that since I'd already had an ectopic pregnancy, there was a small chance it could happen again. For the first few weeks, I held my breath—but still, I dared to hope.

At six weeks, when we got the news that my pregnancy was healthy, the smile on Theo's face could have made even the coldest hearts melt. He wrapped his arms around me and kissed me fiercely, not letting me go until I had to come up for air.

As my pregnancy progressed, Theo became more and more anxious. I could tell by the way he fussed around me, hovering wherever I went, even ignoring some of the royal duties that had once been a top priority for him. He would fluff my pillows and watch my diet. He wouldn't let me carry anything heavier than a piece of paper, and helped me whenever I had to move.

If I'm honest, his overanxious attention annoyed me—but I loved him for it.

When our baby girl was born, I immediately knew I'd have a hard time keeping her humble. She was destined to be spoiled as soon as she entered this world. Theo held her for hours, only relinquishing her to me so I could feed her. Princess Ariella was doted on by her grandfathers, her uncles, and aunts. She had love showered on her by the entire Kingdom.

Even my mother softened. She got what she wanted when I married Theo, but it was Ariella's birth that made her truly happy. When my mother held Ariella for the first time, tears filled her eyes, and I knew I'd been too hard on her.

She was a mother—just like me. I could understand, now, that she was only doing what she thought was best.

I appreciated it all, truly. I did. We got presents and well-wishes from all over the Kingdom. Luca himself beamed, bringing his own toddlers over to meet the new baby.

But what I loved most were the moments when Theo, me, and Ariella were alone. Sometimes, when the nannies had left and the staff were asleep, our baby girl would stare at us with big, bright eyes from her bassinet. She'd smile, grabbing her toes with her tiny, perfect fingers, rolling back and forth on her back as she giggled.

In those moments, Theo would wrap his arms around my shoulders and lay a gentle kiss on my temple. Everything was quiet, but the whole room would thrum with love. I could taste it on my tongue and feel it in the air. It made everything worthwhile—the turmoil that had surrounded our early relationship, the hardships, and even all the grief that we'd been through. Together, we were stronger. Everything that we'd been through made us better.

Every year, on our first child's due date, we lit a candle to honor our first baby. We never got to meet that baby, but it was the catalyst that brought us together. That child was the reason that Theo and I were able to get over our insecurities and actually confess our feelings to each other. It was the reason we grew closer, that we formed an unbreakable bond.

ARGYLE HAS ALWAYS BEEN my home. It's hard to fathom wanting to leave now, years later, when I've been blessed with a husband and a child that I love with all my heart. I've been able to travel with Theo on royal tours and trips all over the world—possibly even more than I would have been able to do alone.

And singing? Well, singing has become a daily habit for me. I've kept in touch with Prudence Halloway, who often comes to the palace to give private concerts. Princess Ariella has shown an affinity for music, even as a toddler.

I don't have a career as a singer. I'm the Queen, now, so it wouldn't be appropriate. But somehow, it's better. I sing for Theo, for my child, and for myself. I sing because I love it and because it brings me joy, not because I feel like it's the only thing that defines me. There aren't thin-lipped teachers telling me I'm doing it all wrong, or long-haired boys who make me feel uncomfortable.

There's just the love of music, and the need to sing.

Now, as I sit in the palace's library strumming a guitar with my beautiful three-year-old princess dancing in front of me, I realize that I have everything I could have ever wanted.

I used to think leaving Argyle was the only way to be free. That I had to be independent to feel like my own person.

I was wrong. With Theo, I can be myself without having to run. I can grow and learn and live a rich life without needing to leave my home, my family, my Kingdom.

Theo opens the library door and strides over to me, flopping down onto the sofa beside me and slinging his arm around my back. I place my guitar off to the side and nuzzle into his chest, letting out a happy sigh.

Princess Ariella toddles over to the guitar and runs her fingers over the strings, giggling. She glances at the two of us, a mischievous smile plastered over her face.

Theo combs his fingers through my hair, laying a soft kiss on my cheek. "Let's have another one," he whispers. I turn to look at him, surprised. We haven't talked about this before.

"Really?"

"Let's make a baby, Cara. You look hot when you're pregnant."

That makes me laugh. I nudge his chest with my shoulder, shaking my head.

Theo chuckles, then grows serious. "I mean it. Let's have another baby."

As I stare at my husband, my King, my everything, happiness erupts inside me. I nod, laying a soft kiss on his lips.

"Okay," I whisper. "Let's have another baby."

Theo groans, wrapping his arms around me. We kiss, only to be interrupted when Ariella taps us both on the knees. Theo picks her up, laying a dozen kisses on her cheeks as she giggles and squirms in his grasp. Our daughter throws her arms around her father's neck, planting a sloppy kiss on his cheek in return.

Over Ariella's head, Theo's eyes meet mine. His gaze is clear, and bright, and full of happiness. In that moment, I know we'll have more children. We'll fill this palace with the sounds of laughter and music.

Ariella wriggles away from us, running over to the guitar again to pluck its strings. Theo slides his arm across my shoulders and holds me close. He doesn't have to say a word for me to know what he's thinking, because I'm thinking it, too.

It's simple, really—just *I love you, always and forever.*

EXTENDED EPILOGUE

CARA

The long dining table is laden with food, drink, and enough tableware to fill a small store. A palace worker is placing tall, white candles in a candelabra in the center of the table and arranging fresh flowers around its base. It looks absolutely gorgeous. I check on the preparations, nodding to the head waiter as he straightens out a fork.

"Good work, Charles. It looks beautiful."

"Thanksgiving should be wonderful this year."

I smile, turning back toward the door. In one of the palace's formal living rooms, the rest of the family is assembled. As soon as I enter, my daughter Ariella comes tottering toward me. She's two years old and starting to get a quick pair of legs on her. Ariella crashes into my thighs, wrapping her chubby arms around them as she giggles.

She's wearing a light pink dress that she's already managed to rip down the front. The girl is a hurricane—and I love her for it.

Theo smiles, striding toward me as he wraps his arms around me and spins me around. He kisses me tenderly before ruffling Ariella's hair.

He's not helping the whole ripped-dress-hurricane situation.

But when he turns to me and smiles, I don't mind. He's wearing a crisp black tuxedo, and he looks absolutely incredible.

Another hand appears on my back, and I turn to see Luca and Ivy standing beside me. Luca wraps me in a hug, saying a muffled, "Happy Thanksgiving" into my shoulder. Ivy gives me an equally warm embrace. When she hugs me, I get a scent of cinnamon and fresh baked goods. She must have been baking up until the minute she left Farcliff to come here.

"Good to see you, Cara," Luca says with a smile. Both of them are dressed to the nines.

"How was the trip from Farcliff?"

"Uneventful," Ivy responds.

I sigh, staring at the two of them as Dante comes to greet me as well. His wife, Margot, looks thinner than I remember, but from what I hear, she's doing well. Both Luca and Dante live in Farcliff now, and I don't get to see them all too often.

Seven years ago, Luca broke his back, and my whole world fell apart.

Four years ago, I thought I needed to run away to be happy. I hadn't spoken to Luca in years, and I was ready to leave everything behind, until I went on a fateful sailing trip with the future King.

A few months later, I promised myself to Theo forever.

Three years ago, Luca met Ivy, forgave us, and came back into the family.

Now? Things are almost too good to be true. We have a two-year-old baby. Luca and Ivy have beautiful twins, and Dante has a daughter of his own. Our lives have changed so much in such a short amount of time. My heart is so full, it feels like it's going to explode.

Luca and Ivy's twins come rushing over, grabbing Ariella's hand and dragging her back to their play area. The three of them giggle as Hope—Dante's daughter—hands them each a toy.

I settle into a seat next to Theo, not even trying to wipe the smile off my face.

It feels good to be a family again.

All heads turn toward the door to the living room as my father bursts through. He stands there, spreading his arms wide, a smile beaming over his face.

Ariella squeals, sprinting toward her grandfather. He laughs as he picks her up, throwing her in the air. She flies up so high I screech in terror, which makes my father laugh even more.

I know where she gets the hurricane gene.

My six sisters and my mother stream in behind him, and all the hellos and how-are-yous are exchanged. Their husbands are here, and ten of my nieces and nephews as well. Nearly three dozen of us are here, ready to celebrate family.

The noise in the room swells as royal waiters pass around drinks and canapés. I have trouble focusing on conversations, because all I can do is look around the room at all the people I love, gathered in one place.

It doesn't happen very often.

How did I ever think I would survive out in the world on my own? This is where I'm happiest. When I'm surrounded by a big family. When everyone is talking at once, and I feel like I can't hear myself think. When there are kids running through everyone's legs, and the scent of Thanksgiving food is already wafting through the palace.

When the maître d' comes to bring us to the dining room, Theo hooks his arm into mine and leads the way. For once, I don't feel like a Queen. I don't feel like I need to act with stiff propriety and make sure my facial expression is appropriate for the occasion.

Today, it's intimate.

We head to the dining room just in time to see one of the waiters trip over his own feet and splash red wine all over the crisp, white tablecloth. Ariella starts giggling. Coco and Hazel, Luca's twins, run forward, eyes wide. They stop just on the edge of the mess as three waiters move to start cleaning up.

Theo tries to help, but he nudges the table hard enough to knock over a few glasses. They smash against the fancy, special-occasion plates, sending glass clattering across the table.

"Shit," he says under his breath, which makes the kids inhale in shock.

I try to usher them away, but the rest of our family is trying to get inside the dining room.

"Turn around!" I call out to the small crowd as my dear family stretches their necks to see the carnage.

Then, it happens.

I didn't even know 'it' was a possibility, until now. I thought we were coming in here to have a pleasant, joyous meal as a family, where we'd catch up and congratulate each other on how wonderful our lives are.

I was wrong.

Because in the chaos of trying to contain the children from heading toward the broken glass and spilled wine, I bump into Theo, who bumps into the table again.

This nudge is harder than the first time. Hard enough to

knock over a tall, beautiful candle that was part of the ornate centerpiece.

If we were lucky, the candle would put itself out as it hit the table.

Are we lucky, though?

No. No, we are not.

The candle hits the wine-soaked tablecloth and with a low *whoosh*, ignites it. A scream sounds out, and I realize after a split second that it came from me.

Theo rushes forward, grabbing a cloth napkin as if to put out the blaze with his scrap of material. He waves it at the fire, trying to stamp it out, but the napkin catches fire instead.

More shouts. More screams. The smoke billows up, and I push our family backward. Dante shouts something. Ivy screams at everyone to back up. My father stands in the doorway, watching for a moment before turning into a human fire alarm. He picks up one of my nieces and a nephew under each arm, carrying them out of the room as he commands everyone to back away.

"Get away from the fire!" I scream to Theo as Ariella cries. I grasp her hand so hard I know I'm hurting her, but I'm not letting go for anything. She's wriggly, she's fast, and she's not going anywhere near that blaze. I haul her into my arms as she flails and screams.

Three staff members come rushing inside. Two of them are carrying bright red fire extinguishers. The fire has spread to half the table, igniting all the napkins, flowers, the tablecloth, and even catching on some of the dining chairs. The smoke is billowing in thick, black waves.

Grabbing the edge of my once-gorgeous gown, I cover Ariella's mouth to protect her. Luca scoops up Coco and Hazel, screaming at the crowd of family members to back up.

The staff members point the fire extinguishers and pull the trigger at the base of the fire.

Thick, white foam comes flying out of both nozzles, smothering the fire in just a few seconds. The foam covers Theo from head to toe, and I turn around to shield myself and Ariella from the mess.

Silence and shock settles on the room. I stay huddled over Ariella, who finally, *finally* has stopped moving. She stares up at me with wide eyes. Her little chubby fingers cling onto my shoulders as I struggle to catch my breath.

Theo wipes the white foam from his face, flinging it toward his feet.

"Your Majesty..." The waiter who spilled the wine drops his head. His lower lip is trembling.

"It's all right," Theo says with a sigh. He glances at me as a flash crosses his eyes.

"Don't you dare laugh, Theo. Don't. You. Dare."

"You have to admit, it's kind of funny—"

"I don't have to admit a thing," I snap. I stand up, cradling Ariella in my arms.

Theo brushes fire extinguisher foam off his tuxedo with a sigh. Charles, the head waiter, rushes over with a white, fluffy towel to help dry down the King. I shake my head, letting my eyes drift over the carnage.

Half of the dining table is still perfect. Pinterest-worthy. Pristine.

The other half?

Decimated. The tablecloth is completely charred, and the table underneath is ruined, too. Most of the chairs have char marks on them, and the dishes and crystal glasses have all turned black.

"Your Majesties, we can prepare the ballroom for a meal, but it'll take about an hour."

Theo shakes his head. "Let's just use the informal dining room. The regular tableware will be fine. No need for center-pieces or anything flammable. No candles."

He flashes a smile at me, and I glare. "Don't even start, Theo."

"I'm just taking precautions."

Ariella stares at her father, and she lets out a little giggle. Theo grins. I try my best not to smile, but deep down, I'm not mad.

No one got hurt. Accidents happen.

I carry Ariella back to the living room where my large, boisterous family are already cracking jokes about the fire. They've blown out all the candles in the room, as a precaution—or maybe as a joke. Either way, I'm grateful.

I put Ariella down, and she immediately runs toward her cousins.

Sinking down into a chair, I shake my head. "That was so dangerous."

"Cheer up, Cara," Luca laughs. "At least we got to see the King of Argyle sprayed head to toe by a fire extinguisher!"

When Theo appears in the doorway with an ear-to-ear grin on his face, somehow looking showered and immaculately dressed again, the room erupts in applause.

"A+ for entertainment, Your Majesty," Dante calls out. "Best Thanksgiving so far."

"Don't encourage him," I shoot back, but I can't keep the smile off my face.

"Don't encourage me?" Theo says in mock outrage. "Babe, I'm a hero. Did you see what I did with that napkin?"

"Nearly burned your fingers off? Yeah, I saw."

Theo laughs, wrapping his arms around me and planting a thousand kisses on my neck. He holds me close until I relent and hug him back. When he stares into my eyes, I see so much love and devotion that it's hard not to smile.

"I'm sorry I scared you," he says softly, touching his nose to mine.

"It was an accident," I sigh. "No one got hurt."

"Nothing like a bit of adrenaline to get the appetite going." He grins. "And to get something else going." His hand drifts down to the small of my back, pressing me against the growing bulge in his pants. Heat sparks in the pit of my stomach.

I blush, shaking my head. "Not now, Theo. You're unbelievable."

"So I've heard." He wiggles his eyebrows, and this time I have to laugh. My husband wraps his arms around me and kisses me tenderly, holding me until I let out a sigh.

"I was so scared you'd get hurt," I say in a small voice.

"I know." He kisses my forehead. "But I'm fine."

"Let's just get through the rest of the day without any disasters, yeah?"

Theo chuckles, his arms still firmly wrapped around me. "I can't make any guarantees. But I can promise I'll make it up to you as soon as we're alone."

Theo kisses me once more and then releases me with a wink.

"Love you," he whispers.

The man must have a spell on me, because all my anger and fear has somehow dissipated.

"I love you too, Theo, even though you drive me crazy sometimes." I turn to the rest of the family and shrug. "Happy Thanksgiving, I guess."

Theo laughs and grabs a glass from a waiter's tray. "Happy Thanksgiving!"

I sigh, trying to hide the smile on my face. This is my

family, and for better or worse, I love them with all my heart.
Flaws, fire hazards, and all.

~

LILIAN MONROE
LONE PRINCE
ROYALLY UNEXPECTED: BOOK SEVEN

LONE PRINCE

ROYALLY UNEXPECTED: BOOK 7

1

———

ROWAN

MY GRANDMOTHER SHOULD BE HERE. She said she'd meet me at the train station, but as I glance around the tiny lobby for the thousandth time, she's nowhere to be seen.

My phone isn't any help. No cell reception. No pay phone either, although there are two little cubby holes where pay phones used to be.

Helpful.

Not.

Grandma did warn me this place was isolated, but as wind howls against the shuttered windows, and a gust of cold air rushes under the doorway, I already know this corner of the Kingdom of Nord is wilder than I expected.

I grew up in Farcliff, a small kingdom nestled between the United States and Canada. It's no tropical paradise, but compared to the subarctic Kingdom of Nord, Farcliff is positively balmy.

Grandma is from Nord. Born and raised. My mother, too, until she had me. Fell in love with a man from Farcliff and followed him south, only to find out he had a whole other family and wanted nothing to do with us. Mom still stayed in

Farcliff, though, so that's where I grew up. Technically, I have Nordish blood running in my veins. I should feel at home here, on some level. Right now, though? I feel very much like an outsider. Like the weather itself is trying to tell me to leave.

And this particular train station? The last stop on the line?

Well, let's just say I should have brought warmer clothes. The Summer Palace rests on the edge of the Arctic Circle, and even at the end of September, it's freezing up here. Apparently, they call it the Summer Palace because the land is almost uninhabitable in the winter, but for two or three months in the summer, it's the most beautiful place on the planet.

I thought I'd be safe at the end of September. The plan was to get in, get the pictures and information I need for work, spend some time with my grandmother, and get out before the winter sets in.

You could say things aren't exactly going to plan.

Nord is currently in the midst of the coldest, stormiest autumn in recorded history. The biggest storm the locals have ever seen is on the way, if I'm to believe what I overheard from other passengers. Even luckier for me, it seems my grandmother has completely forgotten about me.

It's not like her. I chew the inside of my lip, trying not to let worry consume me.

It'll be fine. She'll show up and bring me to the palace. Grandma and I will have the place mostly to ourselves, except for a few staff. I won't have to deal with the rigamarole of a royal prince or princess with all the pomp and ceremony that surround them. Just some quality Rowan-Grandma time, as well as the peace and quiet I need to do my work.

That is, if I actually make it to the palace. So far, my

journey seems to have hit a dead end at the last stop on a long train line.

I rub my hands over my arms, sucking in a breath of air. No matter how long I stare at the train station entrance, Grandma isn't walking through it.

Not exactly the welcome party I thought I'd get. I'm Nord's new lead architect on the redesign of the Summer Palace. I've spent the past year working on this project, dedicating every resource at my own architecture firm to it, and this is my first site visit to put the finishing touches on my design. I wasn't expecting a red carpet, but they could have at least sent a taxi.

Sighing, I do another lap of the room.

Still no Grandma.

I should have stayed in Farcliff. My architecture practice is well-respected and multi-award-winning. It's steady, comfortable work, and there's lots of it. I mostly design houses for the Farcliff elite—of which there are many. My office building also has central heating, a fact that I never quite appreciated as much as I do now.

But I became an architect to create beautiful, important buildings, and I couldn't turn this project down. How many architects get to work on a royal palace in a foreign kingdom? How many architects get to make a name for themselves so early in their career?

The wind bangs against the door, mocking me. My teeth rattle. Does this rickety old station not have any insulation?

The few passengers that disembarked with me at the station have long since disappeared, tucking their chins in their chests and braving the bitter weather outside. I watched them leave, one by one, waiting for my grandmother to toddle through the door. I kept a thin thread of hope alive, picturing her rosy cheeks and happy smile.

As my shoulders drop two hours later, I finally resign myself to the fact that she's not coming.

It's out of character for her. Something isn't right.

Trying to stifle the panic that threatens to well up inside me, I hug my favorite red peacoat tighter around my body. It won't be enough to keep out the cold, but it's all I have.

Balmy Farcliff, remember? They don't sell arctic-proof jackets down there. Plus, I was told the weather wasn't that cold this time of year up here. Google told me a peacoat would be fine.

Um, yeah. *Wrong.*

It's not even October. I can only imagine how much worse it'll get once the real winter hits.

Dragging my small suitcase over to the ticket office window, I bite my lip. A steel roller door has been padlocked over the opening and I haven't seen anyone come in or out of the office behind it.

Still, I knock. I've done it a dozen times already, but maybe someone's in there. Maybe they were asleep. Or busy. Or deaf.

Who am I kidding? It's hopeless, but I do it anyway.

Surprise surprise, no one answers.

A few steps down a dingy hallway, I find a door marked 'Office'. I pound my fist on it as panic rears higher inside me.

Nothing.

I'm alone.

Sucking in a breath, I squeeze my eyes shut.

Stay calm, Rowan. There's an explanation for this. Maybe she forgot I was arriving today?

I shake my head. I spoke to her this morning. Grandma wouldn't forget. She has a better memory than I do, and she's been managing the Summer Palace for over thirty years. Her mind is sharp. She would've sent someone to get me if she couldn't make it to the station herself.

Something is *wrong*. I can feel it in my bones—although that might just be the cold making my skeleton tremble.

Walking back out to the main station lobby, I take a deep breath. The place looks like it's about two hundred years old. Thick, stained glass windows are set high in the walls, and crumbling mortar is sandwiched between discolored bricks. The tiled floor has a worn-out strip through the center of the lobby, where passengers have walked from the front door to the platform.

And most importantly, there's not another soul in here.

Just me and my inadequate jacket.

I could sleep in the train station and wait for the staff to arrive tomorrow morning. That's probably the safest thing to do, isn't it? Wait here, where there's shelter?

Maybe Grandma just got delayed. Maybe she's on her way, but the storm outside held her up.

I should stay.

But what if she's just outside? There could be a taxi waiting for me, or a royal vehicle ready to take me to the palace. Or maybe someone outside will be able to help. One of the locals. They could point me in the direction of the palace. Give me a ride. Call a taxi for me. *Anything.*

A cold draft snakes around my legs, and I curse myself for wearing a dress. My tights may be thick, but they're no match for the cold. I thought I'd be in a warm train, then a warm car, then a warm castle. This is my first time in Nord since I was an infant, and my only chance to make a good first impression. Dress to impress, they say.

Ha.

Dress to freeze to death, more likely.

If I stay in the lobby, will I even survive the night? I lift my chin and exhale, watching my breath dissipate in a white puff before me.

It's frigid in here.

I need to find some help.

Glancing at my phone once more, I lift it up above my head to try to get a signal. Nothing. I open the messaging app to try to sneak a message through to my grandmother, but it bounces back as soon as I hit *send*.

When I click out of the message screen, I see the very last message I received while I was on the train. My ex-boyfriend of six months sent me a nasty slew of insults at three o'clock in the morning last night. Drunk, probably.

Gerry: Don't expect me to be waiting here when you get back, Rowan. Enjoy Nord. It's as cold as your fucking heart.

I read the message for the thousandth time, my fingers squeezing my phone so tight my nail beds turn white. My eyes prickle. For the first time since I left Farcliff, I want to cry.

Gerry and I were supposed to get married—but then he told me he wanted me to stay at home once we were husband and wife. He told me he expected me to leave my career behind to care for our future children. He expected me to be a housewife.

Don't get me wrong, there's nothing wrong with being a housewife. My mother was a single mother who worked hard and also happened to be a damn good homemaker. She was an angel, and she died with no one but me by her side.

She took care of me like it was her sole purpose in life, and sometimes I wonder if she would've been better off without me. After all, I wasn't anything but a burden to her, from the time I was born to the time she died. She could have moved on if not for me. Maybe even lived longer instead of working herself to death for my sake.

When she died, I vowed I'd never again be a burden to anyone. I promised myself I'd be able to stand on my own two feet and support myself.

My work is my life. I started my architecture firm when I was twenty-seven years old, and I've spent the last six years working my ass off to make a name for myself. I'm supposed to give that up for Gerry, or some other guy who wants to be the hero who supports me?

Please.

I don't want to do laundry for four hours a day while I wait for my husband to come home. I don't want to feel like he needs to take care of me—that I'm relying on him for my survival.

No, I want to sit behind a desk and make my designs come to life. I want to win every architecture award there is to win and leave a legacy when I go.

Independence, in every sense of the word. That's what I want. Not that I want to die alone or anything—but I don't want to feel like I'm dead weight being dragged around by my future partner.

So when Grandma told me about the redesign of the Summer Palace in Nord, I applied. I didn't tell Gerry, but why would I? It's my company. My name on the wall. My initials on the company letterhead.

It wasn't until I got the official contract of employment that I told him about the offer.

Gerry didn't take it well. He gave me an ultimatum—told me it was the job, or him.

Didn't think I'd choose the job. Did he ever really know me?

That was a year ago, and we struggled along for another six months before calling it quits. I still get the occasional drunk dial, just to remind me that I'm a terrible excuse for a woman.

As I glance around the deserted train station and hug my jacket closer to my body, I'm starting to miss the warmth of his arms. It was comfortable, at least. Maybe this was a mistake. Maybe Gerry was right, and it's better to stay home and have a gaggle of children.

Steeling myself against the weather, I head for the lobby doors. Against a gust of wind, I push open the heavy, metal door and step outside.

It's worse than I expected.

Cold air slaps me across the face. My eyes water. It hurts to breathe, like a million icy daggers stabbing my lungs. I duck my head against the wind, sucking in a breath as I flip my collar up to try to protect my face from the cold.

It doesn't help. The wind is vicious.

My heart hammers. I take another step, dragging my suitcase out of the train station and finally lifting my eyes to look at the scene in front of me.

If it weren't so cold, it would be beautiful.

A thick blanket of snow covers everything, from individual tree branches to tall, gothic-inspired streetlights. The roads have been cleared, but the harsh wind carries gusts of snow and ice across the black asphalt. They look like thin sheets of white crystals whipping across the pavement.

Straight ahead, at the end of a long, black road, is the Summer Palace.

Against the white backdrop, it looks huge, dark, and imposing. I've seen pictures of it, of course. I've studied the two tall towers that frame the castle on either side and seen details of the arched doors that lead to the entrance hall.

But even from this distance, I can tell the palace is bigger and gloomier than I'd anticipated. I shiver.

At least I don't need directions.

Down a street to my right, a car turns a corner and moves out of view, the sound of the engine muffled by the wind and snow.

Then, a louder noise.

The lobby door shuts with a bang, carried by a particularly strong gust of wind. A latch clicks, and my panic cranks higher.

"No!" I stumble to the door, yanking. My fingers feel like wood. They're not working properly. I claw at the door handle, my fingers sticking to the cold, frosty metal. I peel them away, wincing. If I grab that handle too hard, I'll lose a layer of skin.

My heart jumps to my throat. Wrapping my hand in my scarf, I grab the door again. It won't budge. I pull and pull and pull, trying to pull the door open as tears fall from my eyes and threaten to freeze on my cheeks.

I'm locked out.

No, no, no!

Leaning my forehead on the door, I stifle a sob.

I'm going to die here. I'll freeze to death two miles from the castle.

Where the hell is Grandma?

This was supposed to be the greatest project in my architecture career. It was supposed to catapult me to international recognition. My crowning glory.

Now?

I might die before I make it to the front gate.

Unzipping my suitcase, I reach my stiff, cold fingers inside and dig around for my second hat and scarf. My fingers feel the knitted material of my warmest sweater, curling around it and yanking.

I pull the clothing out of my suitcase and huddle beside

the building to use whatever shelter it'll provide against the wind.

Which is not much, by the way. The wind feels like a claw that reaches through my jacket and scrapes sharp nails across my skin.

Then, with a deep breath, I strip my favorite (useless) red peacoat off, and throw my sweater on over my dress. The wind slaps my skin. I inhale sharply. It hurts to breathe. The air is too cold. It attacks every exposed inch of me, invading my lungs and showing me just how fragile my life really is.

My jacket goes back on, followed by the scarf and hat, then a second scarf and a pair of gloves.

It's slightly better. Still cold, but better.

Sighing, I try the door one last time. Just in case.

Nope. Didn't magically unlock itself.

This is a type of cold I've never felt before. It's an attack. Like the weather is on the offensive, and I'm caught in a battle I wasn't prepared to fight.

My gloves take the worst bite of the wind away as I drag my suitcase down the half-dozen steps and onto the snow-covered sidewalk. I shove my chin into my double scarves, keeping my eyes on the little patch of ground in front of me.

My brand-new, fancy, leather ankle boots slip on the hard-packed snow and ice. I pause, legs shaking like a baby deer, lifting my eyes to stare at the long, dark, bleak road in front of me.

I know how far it is. I've seen the topographical maps and studied the drawings of the area already.

Just over two miles. In Farcliff, it would take me, what, thirty minutes? I wouldn't blink at having to walk that distance.

But now? With the wind finding every weakness in my

jacket, with nothing but a pair of tights on my legs, with unlined boots on my feet?

Two miles seem like the end of the earth, and my destination doesn't look very friendly.

Glancing down the road where the car disappeared, I shudder. The nearest town is twenty miles in the opposite direction. There's a grocery store beside the train station that looks dark and definitely locked, and there are a handful of homesteads between here and the nearest town. There's no guarantee I'll meet someone along the way, so shouldn't I choose the closest option?

My eyes follow the long, straight road that leads to the Summer Palace. It looks...cold.

The alternative to walking those two miles to the castle is standing still, which is a death sentence. I have no choice.

Tucking my chin in my chest, I start the long walk to the Summer Palace, hoping I won't freeze to death before I get there.

~

ALSO BY LILIAN MONROE

For all books, visit:

www.lilianmonroe.com

<u>Brother's Best Friend Romance</u>

Shouldn't Want You

Can't Have You

Don't Need You

Won't Miss You

<u>Military Romance</u>

His Vow

His Oath

His Word

The Complete Protector Series

<u>Enemies to Lovers Romance</u>

Hate at First Sight

Loathe at First Sight

Despise at First Sight

The Complete Love/Hate Series

<u>Secret Baby/Accidental Pregnancy Romance:</u>

Knocked Up by the CEO

Knocked Up by the Single Dad

Knocked Up...Again!

Knocked Up by the Billionaire's Son

The Complete Unexpected Series

Yours for Christmas

Bad Prince

Heartless Prince

Cruel Prince

Broken Prince

Wicked Prince

Wrong Prince

<u>Fake Engagement/ Fake Marriage Romance:</u>

Engaged to Mr. Right

Engaged to Mr. Wrong

Engaged to Mr. Perfect

Mr Right: The Complete Fake Engagement Series

<u>Mountain Man Romance:</u>

Lie to Me

Swear to Me

Run to Me

The Complete Clarke Brothers Series

<u>Extra-Steamy Rock Star Romance:</u>

Garrett

Maddox

Carter